May the Best Twin Win

by Belle Payton

Simon Spotlight

New York London Toronto Sydney New Delhi

SIMON SPOTLIGHT
An imprint of Simon & Schuster Children's Publishing Division
1230 Avenue of the Americas, New York, New York 10020
This Simon Spotlight edition May 2015
Text by Sarah Albee
Cover art by Anthony VanArsdale

For information about special discounts for bulk purchases, please contact Simon & Schuster Special Sales at 1-866-506-1949 or business@simonandschuster.com.
Designed by Ciara Gay
The text of this book was set in Garamond.
Manufactured in the United States of America 0415 FFG
10 9 8 7 6 5 4 3 2 1
ISBN 978-1-4814-3134-7 (pbk)
ISBN 978-1-4814-3135-4 (hc)
ISBN 978-1-4814-3136-1 (eBook)
Library of Congress Catalog Card Number 2014945737

CHAPTER ONE

"Hey, Emily! Hey, Lindsey!" Alex Sackett waved at her two friends, who were weaving their way through the crowded hallway in her direction. "Wow, they look super excited about something!" Alex said to her twin sister, Ava, whose locker was right next to hers.

Ava grinned and slammed her locker closed before the clutter inside could spill out. "Whatever it is, I'm sure it's important, like a sale on makeup," she joked, hoisting her backpack onto her shoulder. She was already thinking about her upcoming Spanish class and wondering if she had her homework with her. Had she left it at home?

"Don't joke. It probably has to do with Homecoming!" said Alex.

Emily Campbell and Lindsey Davis stopped on either side of Ava and linked arms with her.

"Ava! Just the girl we wanted to see!" said Emily breathlessly.

Alex frowned.

This sudden attention alarmed Ava, but she tried to make a joke out of it. "Uh, hi, guys. I realize that Alex and I are identical twins and all, but *she's* the twin you want to see," she said.

"What? No! I mean, no offense, Alex," said Lindsey, barely glancing at Alex. "But actually, it's *you* we were coming to find, Ava, because we want to make sure you're signing up for the big game."

"What big game?" asked the twins at the exact same time.

"The Powder Puff football game?" prompted Emily, as though it were the most obvious thing in the world. And Ava noticed that even though Alex had also asked, Emily still addressed her response to Ava.

"Powder *what*?" asked Ava. This did *not* sound like something she'd be interested in.

"*I* know what it is," Alex jumped in. "It's a

flag football game, and it's all girls. We talked about it in student government on Monday. Next Wednesday, the seventh-grade girls play one game and the eighth-grade girls play another. Then the winning seventh- and eighth-grade teams play each other at the big pep rally on Friday. It's a Homecoming thing they do every year to raise money for the local soup kitchen."

Ava could see where this was going. No wonder Emily and Lindsey were interested in her, not Alex. Alex was not known for her athletic prowess, whereas Ava was the one and only girl on the Ashland Middle School football team.

"Do they have to call it 'Powder Puff'?" asked Ava, wrinkling her nose. "That sounds so last century."

Lindsey laughed. "It's just the traditional name for it. But trust me: It's a serious game. We always raise a ton of money."

"And it won't interfere with your football," Emily added quickly. "We only have one practice, this Sunday afternoon."

"This is going to be so fun!" Alex chimed in brightly. "For once I'll get to be on the same team as my twin!" Ava knew that tone of her sister's—Alex was feeling left out.

Ava noticed that Emily and Lindsey exchanged a quick look, just a flick of their eyes. She also noticed that Alex didn't seem to have noticed.

"Well, ha-ha, you *probably* will be," Emily said to Alex. "Coach Jen appointed Lindz and me to pick one team, and Rosa and Annelise are picking the other."

"We're not the captains or anything," Lindsey added quickly.

"And after people sign up, we flip a coin to see who gets first pick," continued Emily. "Then we just take turns choosing until everyone is on a team. We're getting together tonight to choose the teams, and they'll be posted tomorrow morning."

Ava gulped. Would Alex's friends be loyal to Alex and choose Alex, or would they be more interested in choosing talent? Ava thought she knew the answer, and she didn't think Alex was going to be very happy about it.

"The sign-up sheets are outside the gym," said Emily to Ava. "Don't forget!"

"I won't," said Ava.

"I won't either!" added Alex. But Emily and Lindsey were already hurrying away.

Alex turned to Ava and frowned. "Should we

sign up now? The first bell hasn't rung yet."

Ava shrugged. "I guess."

They found the sign-up sheets just where Emily had said they'd be. The seventh-grade sheet already had fourteen names on it. Ava smiled when she saw that her friend Kylie McClaire had signed up. Kylie had hated football when Ava first met her, but after spending a few of the high school games in the bleachers next to Ava, she now liked it almost as much as Ava did. Ava liked to think it was all thanks to her influence that Kylie now wanted to play on the Powder Puff team.

Ava scrawled her name just below Alex's neatly penned name.

"Are you sure you have time for this?" asked Alex, pursing her lips. "You know you need to keep your grades up."

Ava scowled at her sister. "Thanks for your concern. I think I can handle one Sunday practice and a couple of Powder Puff games without flunking out," she said irritably. But deep down, she knew her sister had a point. She had been diagnosed with ADHD at the beginning of the school year, and she'd been working extra hard to keep her grades up ever since. She had a big science test on Monday that she really needed to do well on, because she was in danger of getting a C. That could land her on academic probation and jeopardize her ability to play on the AMS football team—the *real* football team.

But she had a plan. Today was only Thursday. Her tutor, Luke, was making a special visit to her house tonight to help her with test-taking strategies. She'd study all weekend and then ace the science test on Monday.

Dinner that night at the Sackett house was quiet. Alex had set places at the table for her brother, Tommy, and for her dad, but they were late coming back from practice. The twins' father was the coach of the high school football team, the Ashland Tigers, and Tommy was the third-string quarterback.

"We'd better start," said Mrs. Sackett to the girls. "Luke will be here to tutor Ava at seven thirty."

Thinking about Luke made Alex's face grow hot, so she looked down intently at the vegetarian taco she was assembling. She couldn't

believe how out of control her mad crush on him had gotten! What had she been thinking? Not that he wasn't totally gorgeous, and smart, and funny—in short, a perfect match for her. But he was a sophomore in high school, just like Tommy. Alex knew now that that was too old for her. Whatever. She was pretty sure Luke hadn't noticed how much she'd fawned over him—boys were oblivious at any age, it seemed.

"Have you heard what the committee decided the dress code for Homecoming will be?" Alex asked Ava, as Ava handed her a bowl of black beans. "'Snappy casual.' What is *that* supposed to mean?"

Ava shrugged without looking up from the large taco she was constructing. "You know me, Al. I never let these things bother me. I have you to help me avoid any fashion don'ts."

Alex eyed Ava's football jersey and sniffed. "Well, I wish you'd listen to me a little more often," she chided her sister. "Anyway, I'll do some research about this and find out what people mean by 'snappy casual.'"

"I'll be anxiously awaiting word from you," said Ava.

They heard the front door burst open, and

suddenly Tommy loomed in the kitchen doorway. *Did he grow another inch since I saw him this morning?* Alex wondered. Their Australian shepherd, Moxy, who had been slumbering on top of Alex's feet under the table, scrambled to her feet and barreled into him, her tail wagging like crazy.

Coach slipped past his son and dog and bent down to kiss Mrs. Sackett on the cheek.

"Sorry we're late, honey," he said, plunking down his oversize leather briefcase and stepping to the sink to wash up. Alex was always amazed at how well the orange Tigers coaching shirt complemented his skin tone—how was that possible, for such a bright, garish color? Maybe it was the deep Texas tan he'd acquired in the few months since they'd moved there.

"Are you ready for the game tomorrow?" asked Mrs. Sackett as she playfully slapped Tommy, who was attempting to sit down, and pointed at the sink for him to wash his hands.

"It's going to be an easy one, right, Coach?" asked Ava.

"There are no 'easy ones' in this league, Ave," said Coach.

"Well, easier, then," amended Ava.

Alex didn't know football the way her sister did, but she'd known their dad long enough to know that he never conceded that a game could be easy. She supposed this was a coach thing.

"It's the Homecoming game next week we have to worry about," said Coach. "We have to beat Western if we want any chance to make it to state."

"Oh, I am so excited for Homecoming Week!" said Alex, bouncing up and down a little in her chair. "I can't believe the dance is a week from Saturday! So, Tommy, are you going to the high school dance with a big group?"

Tommy had built himself three towering tacos in a remarkably short time. He picked up the first one, his mouth open wide, but stopped before he took a bite and said, "No. I'm thinking of asking someone." Then half the taco disappeared.

The other four Sacketts stopped and stared at him.

Alex recovered first. "You're going to ask a *girl*?"

Tommy swallowed and glared at her. "No, it's actually a pet armadillo," he said, and made the rest of the taco disappear.

This was big news. Tommy was supercute, and Alex knew lots of girls were interested in him, but to her knowledge, he'd never really reciprocated any of their interest. Or at least, if he had, he had never talked about it. Tommy was funny and playful and pretty nice about driving Alex and Ava places when they asked, but he didn't share much about his love life.

"Who is it?" demanded Ava. "Anyone we know?"

So this is news to Ava, too, Alex thought. She was glad. Sometimes she felt a little jealous of the close bond her brother and sister shared.

"He'll tell us when he's ready," said Mrs. Sackett, with a glance at Coach. "Tom, honey, you're acting like you haven't had a meal in three days. You don't have to eat quite so fast. I'm afraid you'll choke."

He had already polished off two tacos and was starting on the third. "I've got rehearsal in twenty minutes," he said.

Tommy also played piano in a jazz trio in the little time he had off from football. Alex smiled. Tommy's group had gotten tons of attention recently, ever since she'd done a feature story about them for the "Tomorrow's Reporters Today" segment on the local news.

"I need to get ready for Luke," said Ava, pushing her chair back from the table. "I have a big, huge, important science test on Monday."

"I think it's wonderful that you're applying yourself so much, honey," said Mrs. Sackett.

Alex jumped up and helped her brother and sister clear the table. "I need to go too," she said. "I'm going to ransack my closet to see what items qualify as 'snappy casual'—that's the dress code for our Homecoming dance—so I can do an inventory of possibilities."

Tommy grinned. "You do that, Al. And be sure to start a spreadsheet so we can run the numbers later."

Alex knew Tommy was teasing her, but that was okay. He was never a mean teaser.

Mrs. Sackett sighed and put a hand over her husband's. "Well, we did enjoy five minutes of overlap when all of us were together at the dinner table. Not bad for the middle of football season."

CHAPTER TWO

The next morning when Ava and Alex walked through the main doors of the school, they found a crowd gathered in the lobby. Girls were grouped around two lists posted on either side of the doors to the auditorium. Ava pulled Alex over toward the group of seventh graders.

"The Powder Puff teams are posted," said Ava. She tugged at the skirt she was wearing, one of only two she owned. She had taken to rotating them every other Friday, when the football team was supposed to dress up for the next day's away game.

Girls checked the lists for their names and moved away. Ava and Alex joined the line at the back and slowly made it to where they, too, could check for their names. Ava spotted hers on the blue team—it was the first name listed after Lindsey's and Emily's. She scanned down quickly for Alex's name. It wasn't there. Nor was Kylie's.

"I'm on orange," said Alex quietly. "We're on separate teams." She sighed. "Orange is so not my color."

Ava looked at the orange list. Sure enough, Alex's name was at the very bottom. Kylie's was there too, around the middle of the list. "Well, at least you have Kylie on your team. And Annelise." Besides those two, though, the only other name Ava knew well was Rosa Navarro's. Ava cringed. Rosa and Alex were both ultracompetitive and tended to clash a little bit. Annelise was a nice girl, but she was Rosa's best friend, and she seemed easily intimidated by Rosa's strong personality.

They moved away from the group to let other girls check the lists, and walked together toward their lockers. Alex seemed upset.

"Al? You okay?" asked Ava.

"My best friends didn't choose me," she said in a trembling voice. "And I highly doubt Rosa and Annelise chose me on purpose. I must have been one of the leftover players they were forced to take. Did you see how my name was at the very bottom? The least they could have done was alphabetize it. I feel so humiliated."

"Al, this isn't supposed to be a popularity contest," said Ava. "It's just flag football."

"*Just* flag football?" repeated Alex. "It's the game of the year! The entire middle school goes to it! And the team that wins gets to play in the student-faculty championship matchup next Friday during the rally! Your team is totally going to cream ours."

She wasn't so sure about this being the game of the year—after all, the Tigers were almost certainly going to the play-offs—but Ava had to admit Alex was right about her team being more likely to win Powder Puff. She didn't know everyone on the list, of course, but she knew who the better seventh-grade athletes were, and most of them seemed to be on the blue team. She recognized Callie Wagner, whom Jack had told her was a star basketball player, and Edie Traina, the pitcher on the softball team. It seemed like a pretty lopsided matchup. What had Rosa and Annelise been thinking? Maybe they just weren't very good judges of athletic talent. Or maybe they didn't care.

"Still, I don't think people take it all that seriously," said Ava, trying to make Alex feel better. "I mean, how intense can a game called 'Powder Puff' be?"

At lunchtime Emily and Lindsey practically pounced on Ava as she walked into the cafeteria with Alex.

"Ava! Come sit over here with us!" said Emily. "We need to talk strategy—no offense, Alex." She smiled apologetically at Alex.

"Oh! Ha-ha, that's fine," said Alex. "I'll go sit with *my* team!"

Ava could see the hurt in Alex's eyes, but Emily and Lindsey were already dragging her away toward their table.

Ava didn't see Alex for the rest of the school day. They didn't have any classes together, and right after school Ava went to her science classroom to go over some questions on the study packet for the upcoming test with her teacher, Mr. Cho. And then she had football practice, followed by a team pizza party.

She texted her mom to say she would stay at school until the start of the high school game. The middle school was conveniently located next to the high school, so Ava just walked over with her team after their party. She loved getting to her dad and Tommy's games early and watching the teams warm up.

The twins finally met up again just before kickoff. Ava's short hair was still wet from showering, but she'd remembered to pack a clean Tigers jersey that morning, and she'd ditched her skirt for nice, comfy jeans. Alex joined her near the fence, where Ava was watching warm-ups.

"You have to come sit with me," said Alex, without even saying hello first. "I feel like this Powder Puff game is having a polarizing influence on our group of friends. Lindsey and Emily are sitting with Callie Wagner and Edie Traina!"

Ava nodded and followed her sister toward the usual seventh-grade girl group in the stands, smiling to herself at her sister's use of "polarizing." Alex used big words like that a lot. She actually studied vocabulary words in her spare time, which sounded like exactly zero fun to Ava.

Alex's hair was pushed back with an orange headband, and her glossy curls bounced with every step. The Texas weather was finally growing a little cooler, and Alex was wearing her new blue sweater, which was shot through with shiny threads. The bright stadium lights made the fabric shimmer as she walked. *Hmm,* thought Ava. *Maybe I really should let Alex help me assemble an outfit for Homecoming next weekend. She does always seem to know just what to wear.*

They sat with their usual group, but Alex's place between Lindsey and Emily had been taken by Callie. Alex had to squeeze in between Lindsey and Edie.

As Ava had guessed, the game was a blowout. The Tigers pulled ahead 28–0 by the end of the first half. Ava hoped that meant Tommy would get to play.

Most of the other girls were paying little attention to the game. Instead they were talking about what to wear for the Powder Puff game on Wednesday, and who was going with whom to Homecoming the following Saturday.

"Lindz, you and Corey seem to be the only people going as a couple that I know of," Emily pointed out.

Ava, sitting on the other side of Kylie, leaned forward and darted a look at Alex. She suspected Alex still had a tiny crush on Corey O'Sullivan, Lindsey's boyfriend. Would this bother her? But Alex acted unperturbed.

"I think it'll be fun to go as a big group," said Annelise. She and Rosa and Tessa Jones were sitting just in front of them. "If we're still talking to one another after the Powder Puff championship, that is," she added mischievously.

"It's only a game," Alex said with a light laugh. Ava snorted quietly, thinking of how dramatic Alex had been earlier about the game.

"Only a game?" said Rosa. "My older sister told me it's the highlight of the entire year. It's practically a fight to the death. People take Powder Puff really seriously here in Texas."

Is Rosa subtly reminding Alex that she's still a newcomer, and somewhat of a foreigner here in Ashland? Ava wondered. Alex sat back in her seat and appeared to become engrossed in what was happening on the field, but of course Ava knew better than to think her sister was actually paying attention to football.

"Does everyone on our team have a blue shirt?" asked Emily. "It has to be royal blue, not light blue. And we're going to wear navy shorts."

"What color will our flags be?" asked Lindsey.

"I think ours are yellow, and Rosa and Annelise's flags are pink," said Emily.

"I'm thinking we can all wear navy and white socks, too," said Lindsey.

Ava closed her eyes and groaned inwardly. This was their idea of strategy? All she'd heard about so far was what they were going to wear. She looked over at Alex, who was sitting on the other side of Lindsey. Her sister was still pretending to watch the game, but Ava knew perfectly well she was paying much more attention to the fashion conversation that she couldn't be a part of. *Poor Alex,* Ava thought.

At the beginning of the fourth quarter, the Tigers were still up by four touchdowns, 35–7.

"Your brother's going in!" said Kylie excitedly, grabbing Ava's arm.

Ava had seen him too. *Please play well, Tommy,* she thought, trying to channel positive energy his way. He and Coach had been getting along really well recently. Coach seemed to understand that although Tommy loved football, his true passion was music. Maybe his father's acceptance would allow Tommy to relax and play better.

Tommy completed a couple of passes and didn't fumble or throw any interceptions. By the end of the game, the score was still 35–7. Ava let out a sigh of relief that her brother's time in the game had gone well.

"Woo-hoo!" said Annelise. "This is going to be the week for awesome football! Powder Puff, here we come!"

Ava rolled her eyes.

CHAPTER THREE

"Okay, wait. What's a blitz again?" asked Alex. It was the next morning, a bright, sunny Saturday, and she and Tommy were sitting side by side, watching Ava's team, the Ashland Tiger Cubs, play the Lewisville Falcons. Ava was the kicker today. Sometimes she also went in as wide receiver, but Owen Rooney usually started at that position.

"Since when do you care so much about football?" asked Tommy, looking at her with his head cocked sideways. "You're usually down there on the sidelines, chatting with the cheerleaders."

"May I remind you that I am now a football player?" said Alex, a slight frost to her tone. "I'm an offensive player of some sort, and Rosa keeps telling me I'm mostly going to be the decoy, whatever that's supposed to mean. Although I don't know who put her in charge."

Tommy grinned. "Fair enough. Okay, so a blitz is when linebackers or cornerbacks or safeties abandon their usual positions and rush the quarterback when they think he's going to pass the ball. Did you notice how Corey had to throw it to his receiver before the receiver was ready? That's why the pass was incomplete; Corey got blitzed." Corey was the quarterback for the Cubs.

Alex nodded, trying hard to absorb the information.

Suddenly the crowd was on its feet, cheering. Alex sprang up too, trying to see what was going on. "What just happened?" she asked Tommy.

The crowd roared louder.

"Hold on a second!" said Tommy, his eyes still on the field. "He's got this. Yep. Touchdown."

A player on Ava's team was finally tackled, but the top half of his body had already fallen across the end line. The Tiger Cubs fans went wild.

"Explain, please?" asked Alex.

"It was kind of a trick play," Tommy explained.

"Corey handed it off to Greg Fowler—he's number 17, the running back—and he started to run around the right side. But then Greg stopped and threw a long lateral back to Corey, and Corey threw it long to Owen Rooney."

"How come Greg passed the ball to Corey? Can he *do* that? He's not the quarterback!"

"Yes, because it's a lateral pass."

This was a revelation to Alex. But she did know what lateral meant: sideways. "Wow. I had no idea football was so complicated," she said.

"Watch the game, Al!" urged Tommy. "Your sister is attempting the extra point."

As Alex watched, Ava waited for Kal Tippett, the center, to snap the ball to Xander Browning. Xander set the ball down while Ava took two steps, planted, and then kicked it cleanly through the goalposts.

Ava was walking stiffly the next afternoon when she and Alex arrived at the middle school football field for Powder Puff practice. She was still a little sore from her game the day before.

"Ava! Over here!" called Emily, waving her

arms wildly from across the field as though she were landing a plane.

"I guess that's the blue team," said Ava. "So that one must be yours, over there. Yep, I see Kylie."

"Yeah, well, no one's waving their arms like crazy to me," said Alex drily. She sighed. "I guess that's to be expected. But you'd think they'd at least *pretend* to be happy to see me."

"Annelise just waved," Ava pointed out.

"Yes, I'm glad she's on my team," said Alex. "Although she lets Rosa boss her around too much."

"By the way, did I hear you watching football videos in your room this morning?" asked Ava.

Alex shrugged. "A few. I don't want to come across as completely unknowledgeable, considering I'm Coach Sackett's daughter. So I'm trying to learn the basics."

"Looks like Corey's the coach for the orange team," said Ava, gesturing toward the tall red-headed boy with a whistle around his neck. "There. See? He just waved to you too."

Alex waved back. "Who's your coach?" she asked, shielding her eyes with her hand as she peered down the field.

"Xander," said Ava. "But that's fine," she added quickly. "We get along okay now." She shuddered when she thought about how Xander and some of the other boys had treated her during the first few weeks of football practice. They'd tripped her, made her work out in the back row, and even stuffed a mean picture in her locker, all because she was a girl who wanted to play football. Luckily, she'd proven herself to be such a great kicker that their tormenting had ended pretty quickly, and Ava now considered Xander a friend.

"Well, have fun," said Alex.

Xander blew his whistle and beckoned the blue team over for a huddle. "I'm supposed to explain the rules of Powder Puff," he said, and glanced down at an official-looking clipboard. "And then you guys have to elect a captain. And I suggest you don't make it a popularity contest. Pick a person you think knows the game and can lead your team."

Ava felt many pairs of eyes suddenly looking at her, and she flushed. She wasn't used to taking a leadership role.

Xander read the rules on his list. "There are eleven players on each team," he said. "A touchdown counts as six points, and the extra point is two points. You can either kick it or run it. There's a running clock, with two twenty-minute halves."

"What are the flags for?" asked Bridget Malloy. Ava cringed.

Xander looked up from his clipboard, startled. "You're supposed to *grab* them," he said. Then, apparently seeing several perplexed looks, he sighed. "Okay, I guess we need to start from the very beginning," he said. "In flag football, everyone wears two flags tucked into the tops of their shorts. Instead of tackling the person with the ball, you just grab the flag and hold it up so the ref can see it. It prevents a lot of bloodshed and broken bones."

Ava laughed, but no one else seemed to realize he was joking. The other girls were nodding, listening intently. Xander met Ava's eye for a second, and then looked back down at his clipboard. He finished explaining the basics, but Ava tuned out. She looked down the field at where Alex's team was practicing. She saw Rosa pass Alex the ball. It bounced out of Alex's open arms and rolled away. She sighed. She and Tommy had tried to teach Alex how to catch a football many times over the years, but it just didn't seem to be one of her strengths.

"Ava!" her team chorused together.

Startled, Ava drew her eyes away from the orange team.

"Looks like it's unanimous, Sackett," said Xander. "You've been elected captain."

For the rest of the hour, Ava and Xander worked together. Ava took the defense and Xander the offense, and they tried to explain the basic rules of the game. Some of the girls, like Callie and Edie, knew how to play pretty well. Some didn't know anything. Emily and Lindsey both seemed to fall in the middle of the pack.

From time to time, Ava glanced back over at the orange team on the other end of the field. Once she saw Alex attempting a kick. She missed the ball completely. Another time she saw Rosa hand off the ball to Alex and then point down the field, obviously instructing her to run that way. Alex dashed off and promptly tripped and fell down, even though no one was near her. Ava winced.

Corey kept blowing the whistle to stop play and explain what was going on. Even from far away, Ava could see Rosa's frustration with the rest of her team.

Over at the other end of the field, things were not going the way Alex had planned. Rosa passed the ball to her, but the pass was *way* too hard—on purpose, Alex was sure. It was like trying to catch a bullet. Anyone would have dropped it like Alex did.

Then Corey had tried her out at kicker. She'd attempted, nicely, to explain that she wasn't cut out to be a kicker, that that was Ava's role in the family, but Corey had made her try anyway, and she'd run up to kick and totally missed the ball. And then they'd set up an extremely complicated play, where Rosa was supposed to fake one way and then hand the ball off to Alex. Alex was supposed to run down the field. She realized she'd never actually had to run with a football under her arm before. It wasn't as easy as it looked in the videos. She was readjusting the ball in the crook of her arm and just sort of lost track of her feet and wiped out.

Is it necessary for Rosa to groan like that? Alex thought.

Corey whistled to call people over.

"Come on, guys! Huddle up!" Rosa called.

"How about if we practice a lateral pass?" suggested Alex. She remembered that Tommy had explained what that was at Ava's game.

"Not now, Alex," said Rosa.

That bothered Alex. Rosa was already acting like the captain, bossing people around.

"We need to elect a captain," said Corey, when everyone had joined the huddle. "And, uh, maybe review some of the rules a little," he added.

Alex glared at Rosa, but Rosa was so busy smiling broadly at all the other people on their team that she seemed completely unaware that Alex was glaring at her.

"I nominate Rosa," said Annelise.

Many of the other girls chimed in with yesses and nods.

Alex wasn't surprised that people wanted Rosa, of course. Rosa had been positioning herself to be nominated captain from the get-go. And Alex was forced to admit Rosa knew the game pretty well. But being captain wasn't just about knowing the rules. It helped to have leadership training. A tiny part of Alex had hoped that being class president might count for something, but obviously the others didn't agree.

Kylie didn't chime in. *But she didn't nominate me either,* Alex thought grumpily.

Rosa was elected captain.

After practice, Ava crossed the field to Alex and Kylie, who were sitting on the metal bleachers, drinking water. Both were red-faced and panting.

"How'd it go?" she asked.

Kylie glanced sideways at Alex.

Alex sighed heavily.

"We have a little team-building to do," said Kylie delicately.

Ava pursed her lips. "Who got voted captain?"

When Alex didn't answer, Kylie said, "Rosa. And she and Alex didn't exactly see eye to eye."

"She thinks she's all that," said Alex, banging her empty water bottle against her knee. "Like, she's always trying to run things. Just because she got elected captain, she thinks she's Vince Lombardi."

Kylie shifted uncomfortably and glanced at Ava. "Well, it's hard because we only have one practice, and girls are coming at it from all different levels of experience."

Alex harrumphed and crossed her arms. "We didn't learn much at all about plays or anything, even though I kept suggesting we learn one or two," she continued. "For example, the lateral pass. I suggested we practice that. But no one listened to me."

Ava suppressed a smile. Alex seemed so proud of the fact that she had learned what a lateral pass was, and she wanted the world to know it.

"All we basically know is that I'm going to be on offense," Alex continued, "and Kylie's going to be a kicker and maybe also one of the people who runs with the ball and scores the touchdown."

"Whatever," said Kylie brightly. "It's just supposed to be fun. So I'm guessing you're captain of your team?" she asked Ava. Ava nodded.

"Hey, guys!" It was Lindsey, walking with Emily. Annelise, Rosa, Tessa Jones, and Madison Jackson approached from the other direction. "A bunch of us are going to see that new movie *Vampire Cheerleaders*. You guys should come!"

"I can't," said Kylie. "I have to get home and help with the horses."

"Me neither," said Ava. "I have a huge science test tomorrow."

"Oh, Ava, please?" begged Lindsey. "We can go to Rookie's, the ice cream place next door, after and talk strategy!"

"Sorry. I really need to do well on this test," said Ava. "And I still have half a chapter left to review."

"I'll come!" Alex piped up. "The movie sounds awesome!"

Ava gave her a look. Just that morning she'd mentioned how dumb *Vampire Cheerleaders* looked, and how she had zero interest in seeing it.

"Sure, Alex," said Emily with a smile. "But all you guys on the orange team have to close your ears when we talk strategy after!"

She laughed. Alex laughed too, but Ava could tell it was forced.

Alex hated the movie. She hated scary movies, and she hated movies with blood, and she hated movies with totally predictable plots, and this movie was all three of those things. She closed her eyes during most of the worst parts and tried to tune out. This movie had obviously been a planned outing, and she had been asked as an afterthought. Why had she said she wanted to come? Her friends hadn't even seemed that psyched that she was there.

Afterward they walked to Rookie's for milkshakes. The waitress led them to a booth. Alex hung back briefly so she could text her mom, telling her to come pick her up soon, and when she looked up, she saw that the girls had already crammed into the booth—Lindsey, Emily, and Annelise on one side, Rosa, Madison, and Tessa on the other. The booth was really meant for just six people. The waitress dragged a chair over for Alex, but when she sat down, her chair stuck out in the aisle and made her feel even more alienated from the rest of the group. She kept a bright, fake smile on her face, just to show that she wasn't really feeling totally humiliated, even though she was.

"Did Ava tell you we're making her be quarterback?" Emily asked Alex.

"No!" said Alex. "That is so not her position!"

"Yeah, but she's by far the best athlete on our team," said Emily. "So we forced her to. Our basic strategy is to give the ball to Ava and get out of the way."

The others laughed, so Alex did too. A waitress

walked by and bumped her chair, causing her to lurch forward a little. She scooted in as close as she could. She knew she needed to change the subject. "So would someone explain to me what 'snappy casual' actually means for the dance?" she asked them, looking around the table.

"It means skirts or dresses, but not super fancy," said Annelise, twirling a piece of her red hair around her finger. "I'm wearing my sister's blue dress with sequins. She finally agreed to let me! Not to brag, but it's going to look really amazing. And I'm wearing silver flats to go with my mum."

"Your mum?" repeated Alex, puzzled. Why would Annelise bring her mother to the dance?

"Oh, right, can't forget to bring your mum," said Emily.

Emily was bringing *her* mother too? And why was everyone suddenly talking like a British person? She'd heard Emily mention her mother before, but she'd never referred to her as her "mum" until now.

"Is bringing your, uh, mum a Texas tradition?" Alex inquired cautiously.

"Yeah!" said Annelise.

"Totally!" said Emily.

"Absolutely," said Lindsey.

"Oh! Right-o then," said Alex, pronouncing her *o*'s with a tiny inflection of British accent. She kept it subtle, though, since her friends weren't using heavy British accents either. "Then I suppose I'll bring *my* mum along too." It was times like this that made Alex feel like Texas really was a different country.

Rosa had had her head bent down, slurping the last of her milkshake, but Alex saw her raise her head and give Alex a funny look. The corners of Rosa's mouth twitched upward, but she didn't say anything.

Alex glanced at her phone. A text from her mom—er, her mum. She was waiting out front to pick her up. She dug a crumpled ten-dollar bill out of her purse and put it down on the table. "I have to go," she said. "My mum's outside."

The others were back to talking about the Powder Puff game. Alex slid out of her chair and stood up. The ten dollars was way more money than her milkshake cost, but it was all she had, and no one had offered to give her back any change. "Tally-ho," said Alex.

As she was heading out the door, she did hear a faint "Bye, Alex!" behind her. She turned.

Annelise was waving her hand meekly from side to side, and seemed to be the only one at the table who had noticed she'd left. Alex felt her eyes get hot, so she waved quickly back at Annelise and hurried out.

CHAPTER FOUR

When Alex and her mother got home, they found Coach sniffling at the kitchen counter, tears zig-zagging down his cheeks.

"I have yet to figure out a strategy for cutting onions without crying," he said.

Mrs. Sackett laughed and bumped him aside with her hip. "Thanks for helping," she said. She scooped the chopped vegetables onto the side of her large chef's knife and plopped them into a pan warming on the stove, where they emitted a satisfying hiss. The aroma of sautéing onions, ginger, and garlic quickly filled the kitchen.

"It smells so good," said Alex. "Want me to help chop?"

"Your father handled the worst part, but thanks, honey," said Mrs. Sackett. "I'm making curry."

"My favorite!" said Alex.

"My work here is done," said Coach. He kissed Mrs. Sackett on the cheek and disappeared into his study, most likely to watch film.

"Why don't you go upstairs and see if your sister needs a study buddy?" suggested Mrs. Sackett. "She's been at it all afternoon, ever since she got home from your Powder Puff practice. She's working hard for that science test tomorrow—I think she's going to do really well on it. I'm so happy she's been able to take her ADHD in stride."

"Okay," said Alex, heading toward the stairs. She trudged up them slowly and walked into Ava's room without knocking.

Ava was sitting in her beanbag chair, scowling down at her book. She grunted something unintelligible.

Alex was about to flop down onto Ava's bed but stopped to pull the coverlet over the pillow and move a mound of clothes out of the way. Then she flopped. "So what's the test on?"

Ava looked up from her textbook. Her hair

was sticking out every which way, and her eyes looked squinty and slightly unfocused, like a person emerging from a dark movie theater into a bright, sunny day.

"Cells. Animals and plants. It's just so crazy-complicated. None of it makes sense."

Alex nodded sympathetically. "Yeah, I remember when we did that unit in accelerated science a few weeks ago. There are a lot of terms to memorize."

Ava glared at Alex. "I think I remember you studying for it. You ended up scraping by with a ninety-four on the unit test, right?"

"Um, ninety-five, but yeah. I had to study my *butt* off," said Alex.

Ava buried her face in her hands, then raked her hands through her short hair. Now Alex understood why her twin's hair was in such disarray. "I need, need, need to do well on this test," she said, half to herself. "If I don't get at least an eighty, my grade will go down to a C, and if I get below a seventy-five, I could even get a D. That would mean I'm on academic probation. They might not let me finish the football season, let alone try out for basketball."

"That reminds me," said Alex. "I am so not on board with having Rosa in charge of our team. She is totally clueless about football."

"And you're not?" Ava blinked at her.

"Well, there's clueless, and then there's *clueless*," said Alex. "I freely admit I'm not a football expert, but at least I've had a lifetime of exposure to it. I was practically born in the bleachers."

"Which would mean that I was too," Ava reminded her.

"Ave. It's an *expression*."

"I know, sorry."

"Anyway, Rosa, despite not fully understanding the rules of the game, nevertheless thinks that as the captain she knows everything. But she doesn't. And she is *super* bossy." Alex pulled a piece of gum from her pocket, unwrapped it, and popped it into her mouth right before she realized they were about to eat dinner. Oops. "So at one point I said—"

"Al?"

"I said, 'Listen, Rosa. I've been watching videos about how to blitz, and I really think—"

"Al?"

"I *really* think we ought to—"

"Al!"

"Jeez, I'm right here. There's no need to shout. What?"

"I need to keep studying," said Ava gently. "Let's talk about this later, okay?"

Alex sighed heavily. This was definitely not her day for feeling included in anyone's life.

On Monday morning Ava staggered into science class. Her head was buzzing, as though a hive of bees had flown in through her ears. She'd been up until midnight, practicing drawing diagrams of plant and animal cells. There was so much vocabulary! "Plant cell . . . eukaryotic . . . cell wall . . . chloroplasts . . ." She muttered these things under her breath as she headed to her desk and plunked down her heavy backpack. "Animal cell . . . also eukaryotic . . . no cell wall . . . no chloroplasts . . ." Her mind was groggy from not enough sleep, but she felt pretty prepared. Luke had come over for another extra session after dinner last night, and he'd helped her sort out all the strange-sounding terms, like Golgi bodies, ribosomes, and endoplasmic reticulum, until she finally felt like she understood what they meant. Plus, she had that reassuring feeling that if she ran out of time, she could just write Mrs. Hyde's name on her test and then go into her office at lunchtime to finish it. Mrs. Hyde was the school's learning specialist, and Ava had been working closely with her on different test-taking strategies to deal with her ADHD. Getting extra time was one of them.

"Pssst! Hey!" Corey plunked himself down into the desk next to hers. "There's a sub," he said, gesturing with his chin toward the front of the room.

Alarmed, Ava looked toward Mr. Cho's desk. Sure enough, Mr. Cho was not there. Instead she saw a short, heavyset woman in a red dress and black, cat-eye glasses.

"Mr. Cho's daughter had her baby," Corey explained.

"But the baby wasn't due for three more weeks!" said Ava.

The whole class knew Mr. Cho's daughter was expecting Mr. Cho's first grandchild, a boy. He had been telling them excitedly about it since the second day of school. Ava knew the plan—when the baby was born, he and his wife would fly to California to help take care of their new grandchild. He'd planned to be out for a whole week.

The substitute wrote her name on the white-board.

"Mrs. Fowler? Is she Greg and Tim's mom?" Ava asked Corey.

Corey gave her a look. "Yeah, duh. Didn't you listen when Mr. Cho told us that was the plan?"

Ava sighed. "I miss a lot of stuff teachers say," she admitted.

Mrs. Fowler cleared her throat.

Kids seemed not to notice and kept on talking.

She clapped her hands twice.

People continued talking. Ava watched her out of the corner of her eye. She always felt sorry for substitutes. They were either too nice, allowing kids to get away with stuff their regular teacher would never allow, or unduly strict, yelling way too much to show who was boss.

Finally Mrs. Fowler flicked the lights, and the class settled down. She smiled at them. "Mr. Cho told me that tactic would work with you, and he was right!" she said.

Ava noticed Mrs. Fowler had lipstick on her front tooth. She examined Mrs. Fowler more closely. Behind the broad smile, Ava could sense that she was nervous. Ava wondered if this was Mrs. Fowler's first subbing job. She knew that Greg and Tim were twins and that they had five younger siblings. She also knew that Mr. Fowler had been deployed overseas. She wondered who was looking after the little Fowler kids.

Mrs. Fowler was distributing the tests facedown on everyone's desks. "We'll begin in just a moment," she said. "Please be sure all your things are stowed away, and of course, I don't want to see any cell phones. Or X-ray glasses." She laughed lightly, but no one else did.

Ava thought it was bad timing for a teacher to make a joke while handing out a test to a class full of nervous seventh graders. A rookie error, as Coach would say.

When Ava turned over the test, her heart began thumping. The black type swam before her eyes, as though the letters were floating in water. But she took in a deep breath, blew it out slowly, the way her mom had taught her, and focused.

The first part was short answers. Her job was to fill in the blank with the correct cell part based on the definition.

A layer of cellulose fiber that gives the plant cell most of its support: __________

Ha! I know this! She almost said it out loud. She wrote "cell wall."

The jellylike material outside the cell nucleus in which the organelles are located: __________

She knew that one, too. *Thank you, Luke.* They'd studied that one together. She wrote "cytoplasm."

The clock ticked as Ava worked her way through the rest of the test. The only sound was the scratching of pencils on paper, the clomping of Mrs. Fowler's sensible shoes as she made her way around the classroom, and the occasional cough. It was a little weird to have the teacher walking around while they were taking the test. Mr. Cho never did that. He always sat at his desk and graded papers and stuff.

Stop letting your mind wander, she reprimanded herself. She stared back down at the text in front of her and went on to the next question. *I'm not doing too badly,* she thought excitedly. She guessed at a few of the terms, but they were educated guesses.

She read the two short-essay questions and smiled. One was to compare and contrast a plant and animal cell. The other was to explain what a prokaryote was. She *knew* this. Luke had drilled her on prokaryotic cells. Hurray!

And then the bell rang.

"Pencils down, please," said Mrs. Fowler.

Ava hastily scrawled *Mrs. Hyde* at the top of her paper. She'd go to the learning specialist's office during her lunch hour and finish the essay questions.

Mrs. Fowler smiled at Ava as she collected her test.

Just before lunch, Ava and Alex met at their lockers.

"How did it go in science?" Alex asked her, spinning her lock right, left, right.

"I think it went well," said Ava. "I have to go finish the two short essays now, but I know my stuff." She tugged at her locker, but it didn't open. Sigh. One of these days she'd be capable of talking and spinning a combination lock at the same time. She started again.

"That's awesome, Ave," said Alex, smiling warmly.

"Ava!" Emily and Lindsey rushed up.

Alex's smile froze on her face.

Ava wished Emily and Lindsey could be a little less obvious that it was her, not Alex, they wanted to see.

"Hi," said Ava, finally jerking open her locker door with a clang. It had started sticking recently, possibly because she often had to slam it closed in two stages—first at the top, then at the bottom—before its contents could spill out across the hallway. Carefully she opened the door a few inches more, using her knee to stop the books from sliding out. Mrs. Hyde had suggested early on that they arrange for Ava to get a second locker, so that it would be easier to keep her stuff organized, but Ava had thought that would be too embarrassing, especially as she was new to the school.

"We had an idea to discuss with you," said Emily, getting right to the point. "We're wondering what you think about moving Edie to wide receiver, and making Callie a blocker. She is totally the strongest one on the team, and—"

"Sorry, but I can't talk right now," said Ava, slamming her locker door closed again. "I have to go finish my science test."

"No problem," said Emily. "Maybe we can find you at the end of lunch."

"Are you guys headed there now?" asked Alex in her false-cheerful tone that Ava knew well.

Lindsey turned and blinked at Alex, as though surprised to find her standing there. "Oh! Yup. Let's walk there together. But we can't sit with you, because the orange and blue teams are sitting at separate tables again today. For spirit."

"Oh, I knew that," said Alex in that same false-casual way. "I was going to find Rosa and Annelise. Good luck on your test, Ave."

Ava headed off in the other direction, toward Mrs. Hyde's office. She sighed and shook her head. Why did Alex have to care so much about a dumb game? Why would anyone care so much about a game with "Powder Puff" in the title?

CHAPTER FIVE

"Oh, hello, Ava," said Mrs. Hyde as Ava poked her head into the learning specialist's office a few minutes later. "Everything okay?"

"Everything's fine," said Ava, stepping inside. "I just came to finish my science test. I didn't have time to get to the last two short essays."

Mrs. Hyde furrowed her brow and then stood up, shuffling several stacks of papers around on her desk. "Hmm," she said. "Mr. Cho didn't drop it off."

"Oh, that's because we had a sub," Ava explained. "Mr. Cho's daughter had her baby, so Mrs. Fowler—that's our sub—gave us the test."

"Ah, that explains it," said Mrs. Hyde. "Just

run over and ask Mrs. Fowler to drop it off here. She probably didn't realize she was supposed to do that. If you don't have time to finish it during your lunch block, you can do it right after school, and I'll write a note to Coach Kenerson explaining why you were late to practice."

Luckily, Ava's science classroom wasn't far from Mrs. Hyde's office, and luckily, Mrs. Fowler was still there when Ava walked in. Still, she was panting slightly as she explained to Mrs. Fowler the procedure for delivering her test to Mrs. Hyde so Ava could finish it. This was stressful; she wouldn't have much time for lunch, and she did not want to be late for football practice.

Mrs. Fowler frowned. She was sitting at Mr. Cho's desk with a big stack of papers in front of her. *Is she already grading our tests?* Ava wondered.

"I'm sorry," she said to Ava. "Mr. Cho left me no instructions about allowing any students in your class extra time on tests."

"He—he didn't?" asked Ava in a small voice. "Maybe he forgot, because he left in such a big hurry? Because I'm supposed to get extra time, see, and—maybe you could give him a call?"

"A call?" repeated Mrs. Fowler. "I don't think

so, um—Ava, is it? In fact, I think I've already finished grading your test." She thumbed through the pile. "Yes, here it is. You started out quite strong, but I'm afraid you'll just have to learn to work a bit faster. It's probably a better strategy to move on to the next question if you get stuck on something." She studied Ava's test. "Yes, you had twenty-two out of twenty-four on the short answers, but you didn't even start the essays." She held up the test so Ava could see the big red 66 at the top.

Ava opened her mouth to say something, and then closed it again. She stared at the big numbers. That was a D! Her first one ever. Her stomach felt queasy. She knew it was her responsibility to say something, to explain the situation. But she didn't want to have a big scene with Mrs. Fowler. *Maybe I misunderstood,* she thought. This was the first time she'd tried the extra-time strategy for a test. Doubt was creeping in. Maybe she'd just ask her mom about it tonight.

With a slightly quivering chin, she mumbled something to Mrs. Fowler and hurried to what was left of her lunch period.

During social studies, Kylie asked Ava how the science test went.

"Okay," said Ava. "Actually, kind of not great." She started to tell Kylie what had happened, but just then Tim Fowler, who was sitting on the other side of Kylie, leaned in.

"Psst! Hey, Sackett. How'd my mom do today?"

"Oh, ah," began Ava. "Well, she—"

"Because she was so pumped to get this subbing gig," continued Tim. "Since our dad's been deployed, she's been trying to find a steady job for a while. They told her if this science teaching situation goes okay, they'll make her a regular sub at AMS until a position opens up in the district somewhere."

"I didn't even know your mom was a teacher," said Kylie.

"Yeah, she's been certified for, like, ten years," said Tim proudly. "But with all my younger brothers and sisters at home, this is her first time back to work. My grandma's moved in to help take care of my siblings."

Mr. Antonucci clapped his hands to get class started, and Ava slumped down in her desk. This situation was growing worse and worse. How could she tell her mom now? Mrs. Sackett would be sure to call the school and make it an issue, and Mrs. Fowler would probably get in trouble for not following the rules. She might even get fired over this situation.

Should she just take the bad grade? That was the worst scenario of all. First, she had studied so hard for that test. And a D on this test would for sure sink her semester grade below a C, and that would put her on academic probation. Ava couldn't imagine not being allowed to play football when she'd worked so hard to get on the team!

She thought about Luke, her tutor. She tried to imagine the look on his face when he found out what grade she'd gotten. He'd be so disappointed in her. They'd both been so sure she'd do well.

And then an even more awful thought occurred to her. Maybe her parents would *fire* Luke, because he'd failed in his job at tutoring her.

Mr. Antonucci continued to drone on about last night's reading, which had been about Thomas Jefferson and his presidency. Ava had actually done the reading—it had been a nice break from studying—and for once thought it was semi-interesting, but now she was fretting too much about Luke to pay attention. She felt like she was being forced to make a terrible choice: say something to her mom or Mrs. Hyde and risk getting Mrs. Fowler dismissed from a job she really needed, or say nothing about her bad grade to anyone, and risk getting Luke fired.

Suddenly she realized the class had gone quiet and everyone was staring at her. Had Mr. Antonucci just asked her a question? He was frowning at her over his half-glasses.

"Um, sorry, could you repeat that?" she asked him meekly.

Someone tittered.

"The Louisiana Purchase," he prompted her. "Can you tell us a bit about it?"

She knew this. She'd read about it last night. Thomas Jefferson. Napoleon. Westward expansion. Something about Marshall Someone-or-Other. Her thoughts swirled and almost crystallized, and then were gone again, as though she were peering at a pattern through a turning kaleidoscope. "Um, I know Thomas Jefferson had a *lot* to do with it," she said lamely. "I think he, ah, purchased Louisiana."

Mr. Antonucci gave her a pained look and called on Bridget Malloy, who was waving her arm back and forth like a windshield wiper.

Ava slumped back down deep into her chair. Great. She'd probably flunk science *and* social studies.

That evening Alex noticed that Ava seemed preoccupied. She barely said a word all through dinner, moodily mushing down her mashed potatoes and making crisscross patterns on them with her fork. She didn't even want a piece of their mom's amazing apple cobbler, warm from the oven, although she consented to a scoop of vanilla ice cream.

"Ava, do you realize you just put salt and pepper on your ice cream?" asked Alex.

"Huh?" Ava looked at her, startled, and then looked down at her bowl. She pushed it away and sighed.

Mrs. Sackett looked at Ava curiously. "Ave, honey, everything okay at school?"

"What?" asked Ava. "Oh. Yeah. Everything's fine," she said.

"Then how come you've torn your napkin into seventy-five pieces?" Alex demanded.

"Moxy's eaten, like, three pieces you dropped under the table already."

"Let her be, Al," said Coach. "She'll tell us if she wants to tell us."

"Yeah, well, I have some news," said Tommy, who was spooning ice cream on top of a huge mound of apple cobbler. "I'm taking a date to Homecoming."

"So the girl you were going to ask actually said yes? That's awesome!" said Alex. "Now all we have to work on is your lack of interest in current fashion trends."

"There's nothing wrong with my fashion sense," said Tommy.

"You're worse than Ava," she said. *Although girls are probably willing to overlook his flaws,* she noted as she considered her brother thoughtfully. He had big blue eyes, an easy laugh, and good personal hygiene, for a boy. Plus he seemed to be growing taller by the minute. He was now as tall as their dad and looked like he had more to go. "All right, so who is it?"

"Huh?" said Tommy, looking up at Alex as though he'd forgotten what they were talking about.

"I asked, *Who* are you *going* with?" Alex prompted.

"Going with where?"

"Homecoming," she said. He was evidently stalling. *Maybe this is serious!*

"Oh. No one you'd know. A girl."

Alex looked at her mom and dad for help, but they were both suddenly intensely interested in their bowls of cobbler. Alex could tell they wanted to know too but were trying not to push too hard. Traitors. And Ava was hopeless tonight. No, it was going to be up to her to uncover more information.

"What's her name? What year is she?" asked Alex.

"Cassie. Sophomore. She's a friend of Harley's. That's enough questions, Ms. Nosypants."

What was that new vocab word she'd studied just this past weekend? Reticent. That was it. Tommy had become uncharacteristically reticent. Usually he talked a mile a minute at the dinner table, but now his face had gone a little pink as he reached for the whipped cream.

"Tommy's going to Homecoming with an actual *date*," Alex announced to the table, as though this situation needed translating.

"That's nice, Tom," said Mrs. Sackett. "I hope we get to meet her."

Tommy shrugged. "We're going with Luke and Harley. He's driving. It's no big deal."

"I assume you're going to do something about your hair," said Alex. She couldn't resist.

"What's wrong with my hair?" asked Tommy, looking up at her sharply.

"It needs shaping," said Alex. "Just a little around the ears. I can do it for you if you want."

"Ha! No thanks, Al. No offense, but I have no interest in becoming one of your new makeover projects."

"Suit yourself," said Alex with a shrug. "But I've been watching a lot of how-to videos online about cutting hair, and really, it's a cinch. There's not much to it. I've been thinking that cutting hair could be a great side vocation for me to pursue while I'm in college. I'm saving up for some haircutting clippers. But whatever."

"I think it's admirable that you're thinking about long-term goals, honey," said Coach, with a twinkle in his green eyes.

CHAPTER SIX

Ava got her science test back on Tuesday morning. Mrs. Fowler didn't know all their names, so instead of distributing them herself, facedown on people's desks, the way Mr. Cho would have, Mrs. Fowler called out each kid by name so they could come to the front of the class to get their test. According to the plan her parents had drawn up with Mrs. Hyde, Ava was supposed to sit in the front of the room, so she could pay better attention to the teacher. But with a substitute, Ava had seized the opportunity to sit in the back, temporarily, with Corey. It made her feel normal, not like a "special learner."

"Ava Sack*ett*?" said Mrs. Fowler.

The class snickered, and Ava felt her ears getting hot as she forced herself to walk to the front of the room. She'd put the accent on the second syllable. Who in all of Ashland, Texas, didn't know how to pronounce the name "Sackett"? Did Mrs. Fowler really not follow football in this town? If not, she had to be the only person.

Ava didn't even glance at her test as Mrs. Fowler handed it to her. She just clutched it tightly and strode back to her desk, falling heavily into her chair. She couldn't make herself look at that big red 66 again.

She was forced to look at it in detail, though, because Mrs. Fowler insisted that they all go over the tests together. She kept hers close to her chest and didn't put it down on the desk, so no one else could see her grade. No other kids seemed to care much, though. A quick glance to her right told her Corey had gotten a 79. He was scowling down at his test, one elbow on the desk, his chin propped on his hand. That was surprising. *He usually gets high Bs at least,* Ava thought.

A stealthy glance to her right told her that Kal Tippett had gotten a 70. Yikes. It wasn't like he was the world's best student, but he didn't usually do that badly. This really had been a tough test. But still. She'd been doing super well on it. There were only three red marks on the entire first two pages. Then on page three, where she'd run out of time, there were two large red question marks next to the short essays she'd left blank. It was a miracle she'd gotten a 66, she thought.

After class she packed up quickly and was one of the first ones out the door. She didn't feel like having the usual "How did you do?" conversation with anyone.

"Ava!" a voice called to her.

It was Mrs. Hyde. *Just my luck,* Ava thought.

Mrs. Hyde was *never* in the hallways. She seemed to live in her office all day long, or in the little conference room right next to it, in endless meetings with parents and special education officials. Why, today of all days, did she have to be where Ava would run into her? Mrs. Hyde was the last person she wanted to talk to right now.

"Hi!" Ava said, looking down at her sneakers. Kylie had drawn happy faces on the white rubber toes for her.

"Ava, I never received your test from Mrs. Fowler. Should I speak to her about it?"

"No!" said Ava quickly. "It's all good. I—I didn't need any extra time after all."

Mrs. Hyde looked perplexed. "But I thought—"

"Sorry, I have to run to class," Ava mumbled, and hurried past her.

She couldn't concentrate on Mrs. Vargas's practice math problems the next class period. All she could think about was that she was in a lose-lose situation with this science test. Even if she wanted to say something to Mrs. Hyde, it was most likely too late by now—too much time had passed since the test. She ought to have spoken up yesterday. What teacher in her right mind would let her finish the test questions now, after it had been passed back and after she'd had all the time in the world to study up on her answers? Really, the only thing to do was take the bad grade and forget about it. She'd only get Mrs. Fowler in trouble, and might even make her lose her job.

But taking the bad grade was a terrible solution too. She'd get put on academic probation. She might be kicked off the football team. They wouldn't let her try out for basketball. And worst of all, her parents would decide that Luke was doing a bad job tutoring her.

She buried her face in her hands. What was she going to do?

CHAPTER SEVEN

"I mean," said Alex later that night, "I was getting annoyed with my teammates for obsessing about what we're wearing tomorrow, but I think they're right. Pink flags and an orange shirt? What fashion genius came up with *that* idea?" Alex turned from the mirror. "Do you think the pink clashes terribly with these purple shorts?" she asked Ava.

Ava was sprawled on her stomach diagonally across her bed, her hands propping up her chin. She looked up from her social studies textbook and blinked at Alex. "What? What flags?"

Alex let out a patient sigh. Ava seemed to be irritated by everything she said recently. "My flags. For Powder Puff. Remember? Tomorrow is Wednesday? My team plays your team in the semifinals? The winning team plays the eighth grade at the pep rally on Friday?"

Ava rolled her eyes. "Whatever, Al. I really don't think anyone will know or care if your flags clash with your shirt."

"I said my *shorts*, not my shirt, and I think they *will* care," said Alex with some heat. She put her hands on her hips and thrust her chin out at her sister. "What is *wrong* with you anyway? You've been so *cranky* lately."

Ava glowered at her textbook. "Nothing. Everything's great. I just don't really care about the Powder Puff game. Plus, I think it's dumb that they call it that. This is the twenty-first century. It should be called flag football."

Alex started to leave, and then turned and stepped back into the room. "You know what, Ava?" she said. "I think you're being really mean."

Ava blinked at her. "Mean? How am I being mean?"

"You don't seem to know or care that you have zoomed up the popularity charts because of this Powder Puff game. Or that my friends are basically ignoring me because they care a ton about the outcome of tomorrow's game, so they put themselves on your team, and that I have been, like, totally cast aside because I stink at sports. And instead of being psyched, you're acting like this game is something you don't even care about."

"But I *don't* even—"

"And also," Alex interrupted, "you're acting all preoccupied and emo for no reason."

Ava scrambled up to a sitting position. Her green eyes flashed. "No reason?" she repeated bitterly. "You don't know anything about it."

Alex gulped. Did Ava have *tears* in her eyes? With a rush, all her annoyance at her sister vanished, and she stepped over and sat down on Ava's bed, wincing painfully because the corner of Ava's textbook jammed into her thigh. "Ave. Tell me. What's going on?"

Ava told her. She told her about Mrs. Fowler, and how Mrs. Fowler hadn't brought Ava's test to Mrs. Hyde to finish, and what Tim Fowler had said about how much his mother needed the job, and how Ava didn't want her to get fired. She told Alex that by not speaking up for herself, she was stuck with a bad grade, and now

Luke would probably lose *his* job tutoring her.

Alex let Ava finish without interrupting her. Then the two girls sat side by side, chins in hands. *Yes, this is definitely a tricky situation,* Alex thought. Ava was right about that.

The twins remained silent for a few moments.

Then Alex spoke. "Ave, you have to stand up for yourself," she said. "The thing to do is to tell Mom what's going on. She'll straighten everything out."

"I can't involve Mom," said Ava. "It's too late for that. Then Mrs. Fowler will really be in trouble. Even though Mom's really nice and stuff, you know how teachers and principals get. They pay attention when parents start showing up on the scene."

"Then solve it yourself," said Alex simply. "Go talk to Mrs. Fowler and explain the situation more calmly. Maybe she just doesn't understand how the whole thing works. Then she can correct her mistake and won't get in trouble for it."

"But—" Ava stopped, trying to find holes in Alex's plan, besides the fact that the idea of confronting Mrs. Fowler made her shiver. "You're right, Al. That's what I should do." She sat, lost in thought for a minute. Then she smiled. "Thanks."

Alex stood up. "You're welcome. Now tell me if the flag clashes with my shorts."

An hour later they stood side by side in the bathroom, brushing their teeth.

"By the way," said Alex, "I've been studying up on the rules of flag football, and I warn you that your team is underestimating my hidden talents."

"Is that right?" asked Ava, grinning.

"Yes. So good luck to you tomorrow, and don't go easy on me, just because you're my twin."

"Oh, I won't," Ava replied. "I'm very afraid. May the best twin win."

"Actually, you mean, 'May the *better* twin win,'" Alex corrected her. "When you're comparing two things or two people, you would use the comparative *better*, rather than the superlative *best*. You'd use the superlative for three or more things or people."

Ava sighed. "It's just an expression, Al," she said.

CHAPTER EIGHT

On Wednesday they had a special schedule. Every class was shortened by five minutes to allow time for the Homecoming Week semifinal games last period. After that, kids would be able to get to their sports and cheerleading practices on time. The school was a sea of blue and orange—team members were supposed to be wearing their team's color.

Alex had had her orange outfit planned for two weeks. She'd discovered shortly after moving to Ashland that orange wasn't her best color, but she'd found a pretty orangey-coral lip gloss that enhanced her natural skin tone. There was nothing to be done about the shirt—everyone had to wear either an orange or a blue AMS T-shirt—but she'd pulled her hair back and added a pretty orange bow made of a nice, heavy ribbon.

"What are the sixth graders doing for their spirit sport?" she asked Annelise as she joined up with her team in the gym before the game.

"They're doing a tug-of-war," said Annelise. "The winning team gets free ice cream at the game on Friday night."

Alex smiled at the groups of sixth graders laughing and chattering with one another. Sixth grade felt like it had been years ago. They seemed so young to her.

"And where's the eighth-grade game being played?"

"Over at the high school, on their practice field," said Annelise.

Alex glanced at the large gym clock, which was protected from flying projectiles with a metal grid. *Why are we not gathering as a team yet?* she thought. The period was only fifty minutes long. She glanced at Rosa, who was chatting and laughing with Tessa Jones. Okay, sure, her orange team had no prayer of beating Ava's team, but shouldn't they at least take this seriously? It was so hard to resist the urge to take charge, to call the orange team over and deliver a rousing pep talk about team goals and playing with heart. But Alex restrained herself. She reminded herself for the zillionth time that she'd been one of the last players to be picked, so she was hardly in a position to act like the team leader. But still, it was annoying that no one seemed to be paying attention.

"Come on. We need to get painted," said Annelise. She tugged Alex by the shirt across the gym to where two high school girls—Alex recognized one as Kylie's sister, but she didn't know the other girl—were helping to paint the orange team's faces. Everywhere Alex turned, she saw girls with heavy eye black in two half-moons underneath their eyes, plus other things painted or drawn on their faces. Sydney Gallagher had the word ORANGE across her forehead. Madison Jackson had a big pink powder puff on one cheek, and AMS on the other.

Alex submitted to being painted and a few minutes later her face was covered with eye black and blue and orange stars. Even if she couldn't win this game, at least she'd look good playing.

Finally Corey waved his arms to signal to his team to walk out to the field. Scores of kids were lined up along the sidelines.

Alex noticed a clump of seventh-grade boys standing together, shaking pom-poms. A couple of them had loud plastic horns, which they were already blasting.

Corey called their team over for a huddle. Alex smiled at him as she and Annelise headed over. He looked so cute in his orange AMS baseball cap with the whistle around his neck. She tried not to stare at his eyes as she drew closer. Although Lindsey was on the other team, so what did it matter if Alex just admired him a tiny bit? It wasn't like she still *like* liked him or anything.

"So let's do a quick review of the rules," said Corey, getting right down to business. "There are two twenty-minute periods, with a running clock. But the clock will stop for dead balls during the last two minutes of the game."

"What's a dead ball?" asked Tessa Jones. Her face was heavily decorated with dark-black lines and orange stripes. "You mean if the air goes out of it?"

Alex resisted the urge to smack herself

across the brow. She, Alex, might not be much of an athlete, but she'd at least studied up on the rules!

Corey didn't act like Tessa had just asked the dumbest question ever. "A dead ball means play stops; if the ball hits the ground, if the carrier goes out of bounds, or as soon as the other team has grabbed your flag."

Tessa nodded. Everyone seemed to be paying attention, for once.

"So the other team is going to receive the ball, because we lost the coin toss," said Corey. "And Kylie is going to kick it off for us, although I might also use you as a receiver, Ky, because I saw you make a great catch in practice."

Alex had almost forgotten that Kylie was on her team. There she was, hanging toward the back of the huddle. She beamed at Corey. Well, good. Ava had told Alex that Kylie had become quite a football fan.

"And as we talked about in practice, Rosa will be the QB. She's got a good arm."

Alex knew that QB meant quarterback, but she looked around to see if others had figured it out. They were all nodding.

"Alex and Annelise are speedsters, so you

guys set up on the outside and go long. But don't forget to turn around and look for the pass from Rosa."

"What's 'go long'?" asked Annelise.

Corey blinked. "It means run as fast as you can and try to sprint past your defender. Then maybe one of you will be open and can look for the pass. But remember: You have to *catch* the ball. It doesn't count to just let it bounce out of your arms the way some of us did in practice."

The girls all nodded.

Alex caught her breath. Corey had called her a speedster! She hadn't thought he'd noticed anything about her! She resolved right there to outrun her defender, receive the ball from Rosa, and score a touchdown. Her job was to avoid people on the other team who were going to try to steal her flag.

Corey finished assigning positions to the rest of the girls and gave them instructions about how to wear their flags. "Any questions?" he asked.

Alex raised her hand.

"Alex, you don't have to raise your hand," said Corey kindly.

Alex blushed. "Force of habit," she said. "So

I was wondering about lateral passes. Are we allowed to throw those?"

Corey grinned at her. "You're allowed to attempt any number of lateral passes or backward passes, from any point on the field. We're only allowed one forward pass, and it can start from anywhere behind the line of scrimmage."

Alex nodded. "Got it. Thanks."

"Looks like Mr. Kenerson is waiting for us. He'll be the ref today. Huddle up, guys."

Alex watched from the sideline as Kylie kicked off. Her kick was not bad at all. It went about twenty yards. Alex wondered if Kylie had been doing some extra practicing since their practice on Sunday.

Ava caught it easily at the forty yard line and ran up the sideline. Alex watched as Rosa tried to catch her, but Ava darted away, fast as a minnow, and headed toward the center of the field. Luckily, Sydney Gallagher managed to grab Ava's flag twenty yards from the end zone. She held it high above her head triumphantly, and Alex's team yelled and cheered.

Miraculously, Ava's team didn't manage to score, even though they had four chances to go just ten yards. Alex was pretty sure Ava was trying not to be a ball hog. On the first down, she threw a perfect pass to Lindsey, who grasped at it for a minute and then dropped it. On the second down, she handed it off to Emily, who pivoted toward the end line and practically collided with Sydney, who grabbed Emily's flag. On the third down, Lindsey ran straight into a clump of defenders, and Madison grabbed her flag and waved it high.

Alex sighed. Not that she was rooting for Ava's team, but it was obvious that Ava could take the ball herself and run it in with no problem. She could probably win the game single-handedly. But she was Michael Sackett's daughter, and that meant she was a team player. Ava's team was forced to punt, and Alex's team now had the ball.

In the huddle, Rosa told Alex to dash toward the sideline, turn, and look to receive the throw.

"Okay," said Alex, "but don't throw it too hard. I have trouble catching hard throws."

Rosa rolled her eyes. "I'll underhand it to you if I have to. But I've seen you run. You're pretty fast."

Alex's heart swelled. Maybe she did have some athletic ability after all! And maybe Rosa actually knew what she was talking about! After all, she'd recognized Alex's hidden talents.

On the line of scrimmage, Alex waited, poised for the cue they'd practiced.

"Orange eleven!" said Rosa. "Orange eleven! Hut! Hut! Hut!"

On the third "hut," Alex took off at top speed, running toward the right sideline. She turned, saw Rosa looking at her, and held her breath as Rosa sidearmed the ball to her.

Bobble, bobble. She almost dropped it. But then her arms scooped it in, and she clutched it to her chest and took off running.

Before she knew it, the whistle blew. She'd only gone about three yards. She turned.

Ava stood behind her, waving the flag she'd grabbed from Alex's waistline, grinning sheepishly at her sister.

The clump of seventh-grade spectators yelled, shook their pom-poms, and blasted their horns. Alex had no clue if it was because she'd caught the ball or if it was because Ava had grabbed her flag.

So Xander had told Ava to play both offense and defense? That didn't seem right, with so many girls on the team. Whatever. Alex sniffed haughtily at her twin and headed back to the huddle.

This time, back on offense, Ava took matters into her own hands. Emily hiked the ball. Ava looked as though she might throw it to Lindsey on the side, but instead feinted left, jabbed right, and then took off toward the sideline.

No one could catch her. She coasted across the line into the end zone for a touchdown. Then Ava's team ran it in for an extra two points. The score was 8–0.

When it was Alex's team's turn to be on offense, Rosa threw a long pass to Annelise, but Ava flew out of nowhere to intercept it and then ran it back for another touchdown.

At halftime the score was 16–0.

"I thought it would be way worse than it is," said Rosa, wiping her brow with her flag.

Corey was calm but firm in the huddle. "We can beat these guys," he said. "We just need to play our game. Ava's the only one who's a real threat. Defense, we need to be aware of where she is at all times." He looked meaningfully at his defense. All eleven girls stared down at their sneakers. "And Alex—use your speed. Try that cutback move we practiced on Sunday, and go for it."

Alex nodded, although she had no clue what on earth he meant by a cut-back move, let alone remembered having practiced it.

"Yeah, he's right," said Rosa. "Alex and Annelise, both of your defenders are pretty slow. Try to shake them. I'll look for you."

Alex started to say something, but then didn't. Maybe Rosa wasn't just being bossy. Maybe she was actually trying to help the team.

In the third quarter, the orange team finally found its rhythm. Rosa connected with Annelise again at the ten yard line. Annelise spun around to keep the defense from grabbing her flag, and then took off running. No one on the blue team could grab her flag. Touchdown!

Corey set up a simple play for the extra points, and it actually worked. Tessa trotted effortlessly into the end zone. The blue team's defense was still looking around in confusion when the scoreboard ticked from six to eight points.

In the fourth quarter, Rosa faked a pass to Alex and then streaked into the end zone herself. Then she ran it in for the extra points, just barely avoiding Ava's lunge for her flag.

The score was tied. The crowd roared.

When they got down to the final two minutes, the score remained the same. Ava's team had the ball. In the huddle, Corey pointed at Alex. "Go in for Sydney on defense," he ordered her.

"I don't know how to *play* defense!" protested Alex. "We never practiced it!"

"Yeah, but Ava's the most dangerous player on the field. And you know your twin sister better than anyone," said Corey. "You can read her instincts. Figure out where she wants to pass, and go for the interception. You're quicker than you think you are, Alex."

Alex gulped, but she knew Corey was probably right. She *did* know what Ava was thinking, more often than anyone else. But she had no clue whether she could read Ava's thoughts on the *football* field. And yet—Corey believed in her. He was confident enough to risk putting her, Alex, into the game, even though by pretty much all accounts she stunk as an athlete.

As the two opposing teams lined up at the line of scrimmage, Alex stared at her sister, poised to receive the ball. What was her plan? Alex tried to read Ava's thoughts. Then she saw Ava's eyes flick to Emily, just for a split second. That was all Alex needed.

"Blue nineteen!" yelled Ava. "Blue nineteen!"

Alex felt all her muscles coil up like a taut spring.

"Hut!"

The second the ball was snapped, Alex took off like a jackrabbit, hot on Emily's heels. Emily was going long. Alex chased after her. As she gained on Emily, who wasn't actually very fast at all, Alex darted a glance over her shoulder just in time to see Ava launch the ball. She also caught a fleeting glance at Mr. Kenerson, who was huffing and puffing down the field as well, his whistle bouncing as he tried to keep up.

Alex turned and jumped into the air, her arms outstretched. Somehow, the ball landed in her hands and didn't bounce out again. She had intercepted it! She stopped in her tracks and stared down in disbelief at the ball she was holding.

"Run! Run!" yelled Corey over the roar of the crowd.

Alex ran.

"No, no! The other way!" yelled Corey. About three dozen seventh-grade spectators yelled the same thing.

Alex turned and ran in the other direction,

almost colliding with a confused-looking Mr. Kenerson. The thought occurred to Alex, even as she changed direction, that players probably didn't run in the wrong direction very often.

She raced down the field as fast as she'd ever run, totally focused on the end line she needed to cross. And also on not dropping the football, which was clenched under one arm. The sound of the crowd roared in her ears.

And then she saw a flash of blue to her right. It was Ava, bearing down on her.

A sudden flurry of orange spots danced around on Alex's left side. "Kylie!" she shrieked. Kylie had run across the field to help Alex. She'd decorated her hair with orange beads, which must have been what Alex had seen out of the corner of her eye. "Catch!" Alex shouted, and lobbed the ball toward her teammate underhand.

A surprised Kylie caught the football that Alex lateraled to her and took off running—in the right direction.

"Hey, can she do that?" asked an indignant Lindsey. She stopped, put her hands on her hips, and watched Kylie zoom down the field.

"Of course," said Mr. Kenerson as he passed

by her, still huffing and puffing. He mopped his brow with his sleeve but kept running after Kylie.

Alex knew her pass had been legal. You didn't have to be the quarterback to pass it—as long as it was a lateral pass. She smiled, watching Kylie's heels kick up behind her as she zoomed down the field.

Ava must have realized what was happening right away, of course, but she was too far away from Kylie to grab her flag. "Get her flag!" she yelled at Emily. But Emily wasn't fast enough.

Kylie sailed across the end line, six feet away from any defender.

Mr. Kenerson continued toward the end zone, stopped, and shot both arms into the air.

Touchdown. The crowd went wild!

Alex's team had won.

Alex stood there, stunned, as seventh graders stormed the field, waving pom-poms and blowing plastic trumpets. Her team had beaten Ava's team! They were going to the Powder Puff final game on Friday!

CHAPTER NINE

Ava realized Kylie would score the touchdown the second she saw her take off running. She knew enough about angles and speed to understand that no one on the blue team was close enough, or fast enough, to overtake her and grab her flag. The blue team was going to lose. Her team, the heavy favorite, was going to lose. She closed her eyes and took a deep breath. *It's only a dumb Powder Puff game,* she told herself. *Who cares?*

She opened her eyes. That had worked. She was calm. She was already over it. *Good for Alex,* she thought.

The clock ticked down, and the crowd

cheered and honked. Ava headed off the field, already thinking about real football practice.

"Ava!" Rosa and Lindsey were beckoning her over. Both teams, the blue and the orange, were congregating around Corey.

Corey was reading a text to the group. "Good job, seventh-grade orange!" he said. "And this just in: I have the results of the eighth-grade game." Everyone leaned in, and Corey waited dramatically before continuing. "The blue team beat the orange team."

The crowd erupted in half cheers, half disappointed "ohhs" from most of the other girls, except Alex and Ava, who, being new, didn't really know any of the eighth-grade girls yet.

Corey continued, "So this Friday's matchup will be seventh-grade orange against eighth-grade blue. With teachers, of course. And you have to elect a new coach. Xander and I can't coach you guys on Friday, because we have to be on the cheerleading squad."

Ava grinned. A bunch of the seventh- and eighth-grade boys would be dressing up as cheerleaders and performing a routine during the halftime of the Powder Puff final. That would be a sight to behold.

"I nominate Ava," said Rosa immediately.

That got Ava's attention. "What? Me? The coach? I have no leadership skills."

"Yes, she does," said Alex loyally. "Don't believe her. She'll be a great coach. Plus, I think we can all agree she's pretty much the only seventh grader who actually understands how to play football."

The others nodded in agreement.

"So that's settled then," said Corey. "Ava's going to coach the seventh-grade student-faculty team."

Ava opened her mouth to say something, but then shrugged. "Okay," she said. "I'll coach you guys."

"Your first job is to recruit some female teachers to play for the seventh-grade team in the game on Friday," said Corey, looking down at his clipboard. "According to the rules, there have to be at least five teachers and six students on the field at all times for each team."

"But there aren't any decent athletes among the seventh-grade teachers," said Rosa with a groan. "We're going to get creamed."

"And some of the eighth-grade faculty are crazy athletic," added Annelise. "Like Ms. Peterson, the math teacher? She played college basketball." She looked around the group to be sure her words had sunk in.

"And Ms. Santos used to play for the Mexican national team in soccer," said Sydney.

"And my older brother saw Mrs. Burleigh, the eighth-grade social studies teacher, in the weight room the other day deadlifting two hundred pounds," said Rosa glumly.

"I'm not worried," said Alex, twirling her flag casually. "Ava is an excellent judge of talent. She'll recruit the best athletes AMS has to offer. Right, Ave?"

Ava smiled weakly at her sister. "Sure," she said.

Thursday morning Ava got a ride into school early with Coach and Tommy to find Mrs. Fowler alone and speak to her. Maybe they could figure out a way to solve the problem without getting Mrs. Fowler fired, Luke fired, or Ava put on academic probation. Exactly how, Ava wasn't sure. Sometimes adults had a way of figuring out monstrous problems such as this one in ways that never would have occurred to Ava.

Coaching the Powder Puff football team was the last thing on her mind as she knocked softly on Mrs. Fowler's open classroom door. At football practice Greg had mentioned that his mom had been getting to school early every morning, because she was so anxious to do a good job. That had made Ava feel worse than ever.

Mrs. Fowler was talking on her cell phone, but she beckoned Ava in.

"I'm sure it's just teething. Sorry she's fussy. Is she warm?"

She paused to listen as the person on the other end said something.

"She seemed okay this morning. But keep me posted." Another pause. "Thanks, Mom," she said. "I just don't know what I'd do without you." She clicked her phone off and put it into her purse.

Ava remembered that Tim had said his grandmother was looking after his younger siblings while his mom worked. Still, it was weird to think of teachers having moms.

Mrs. Fowler smiled. "Ava!" she said. Ava noticed that her glasses made her look older than she was, as did the streak of gray in her hair near her ears. But Mrs. Fowler had a nice smile, even though tiny worry lines crinkled at the corner of her eyes when she displayed it.

"Um, hi, Mrs. Fowler," she said, stepping hesitantly into the room. "I—I wanted to talk to you about my test situation." There. She'd said it. Now there was no turning back. Ava felt her mouth go dry and her heart pound harder. She stared at the model skeleton standing in the corner near the front of the room, then at the row of jars and beakers on the high shelf along the wall. She looked anywhere but at Mrs. Fowler, this poor woman with so many little kids at home and a husband overseas, the woman who really needed this teaching job.

"Ah. Yes. Your test. I remember that one. What a shame. You started out so strong, and then ran out of time. Next time, just pace yourself and work a little faster."

Ava bit her lip. Part of her agreed with Mrs. Fowler. It did seem unfair that she, Ava, got to have more time to take tests than other kids. But her mom had explained to her that having a learning difference meant she really did have a right to extra time. She started again. "Yeah, I know, but um, that's the thing I came to talk to you about. See, I have this accommodation thing in my file. And it says that I am allowed extra time to take tests because I, um, I have ADHD."

Mrs. Fowler gave a start.

"I—I know I should have tried harder to tell you. I'm really sorry. I hope this doesn't get you in—in trouble or anything."

Mrs. Fowler stood up and reached for a manila folder on the standing file rack at the corner of her desk.

Ava was always surprised by how short Mrs. Fowler was, considering how large her twin sons were—they must have gotten their height and athletic ability from their father. She'd never seen him, because he'd been away since last spring, before she'd even moved to Texas.

Mrs. Fowler pulled the manila folder from the file and opened it, frowning. "You have accommodations? I didn't see . . ." She scanned the list. Then she looked back up at Ava. "You are right, Ava. I am so sorry. Your name is here, but it isn't filed alphabetically for some reason. I see it now, down at the bottom. Oh, dear." She set the file down and drummed her fingers on her chin.

"I'm really sorry, Mrs. Fowler," said Ava. "I didn't want to say anything to Mrs. Hyde, because I didn't want to get you in trouble. I know how much you need this job and stuff. And it's probably too late for me to retake the test, because of course now I would have had time to do a ton of extra studying, knowing what the short essays were about, so I—"

"Ava. Dear. Please," said Mrs. Fowler. "You won't get me in trouble, I promise. I will speak to Mrs. Hyde today. We'll straighten this all out. I do appreciate your concern for me, though. And it's a good learning moment for me. You *did* try to tell me something after the test, and I should have taken the time to listen. I will also speak with Mr. Cho. His grandson needs to have a few tests done, so Mr. Cho will be staying in California another week. But I can handle this. My guess is that he will recommend that we simply give you two new essay questions to answer. Do you have a free period tomorrow?"

"Yes, I usually meet with Mrs. Hyde during my lunch period on Friday," said Ava.

"Perfect. You can plan to retake the end of the test then."

Ava felt relief wash over her. This was definitely one of those times when it was a good thing to share your problem with a grown-up. Mrs. Fowler had already made her feel better.

She blew out the breath she hadn't realized she'd been holding.

"That's awesome, thanks. Um, I hope your daughter feels better."

Mrs. Fowler looked startled.

"I—I heard you say your baby was fussing. I hope she isn't sick."

"She'll be fine, thanks," said Mrs. Fowler. "She just has a new tooth. My mother is keeping an eye on her for me. But you're nice to ask."

Ava picked up her heavy backpack and swung it onto her shoulder. As she did so, her backpack hit a pink eraser on the corner of Mrs. Fowler's desk. It flew up into the air. "Oops, sorry, I—"

A hand shot out, seemingly from nowhere, and caught the eraser just as it was beginning its downward descent. Mrs. Fowler had been half turned away from Ava but must have seen the eraser go flying out of the corner of her eye. She'd executed a spin move, pivoting on her back foot, swinging around toward Ava, and deftly catching the eraser in a lightning-quick maneuver.

She smiled at Ava and put the eraser back down on the desk. "Whew!" she said in an undertone, almost as if she were speaking just to herself. "Still got it, I guess."

Ava blinked. "Wow. That was impressive."

Mrs. Fowler laughed and sat back down to her pile of grading. "I played shortstop in high school. Our team was the All-District champ," she said. "I suppose it's like riding a bike—you never forget."

The wheels were turning in Ava's brain. Now that the test issue seemed to have been resolved, her mind was shifting to her coaching duties, and her recruiting instincts had gone on high alert. "Mrs. Fowler? Would you be willing to join the seventh-grade student-faculty Powder Puff team for our big matchup against the eighth graders? It's tomorrow, during the pep rally."

Mrs. Fowler hesitated. "I'm sure that would cause Timothy and Gregory incalculable embarrassment," she said. Then her smile broadened. "I'd be glad to, Ava."

CHAPTER TEN

Alex was just closing her locker when Ava appeared at her side. She told her twin about her meeting with Mrs. Fowler. "It looks like it's going to work out," she said.

"Oh, Ave, that's great. I'm so glad you decided to talk to her," said Alex, and she meant it.

"And Al, you'll never believe this, but Mrs. Fowler is a total stud. I recruited her for the game tomorrow."

Alex was dumbfounded. "Are we talking about the same Mrs. Fowler? She's so short and so—*rotund*. She doesn't, er, look like she'd be much of an athlete."

"I know, but she has the most amazing hands.

And she's quick! You should have seen the spin move she just executed, catching an eraser."

"So should I help you look for the hidden talent lurking in our seventh-grade female faculty?" asked Alex with a laugh. A noise behind her made her turn.

A group of eighth-grade boys was making its way down the hall, laughing noisily and jostling up against one another. Mrs. Barber, the seventh-grade reading specialist, was just stepping out of her office, followed by a girl Alex didn't know. The girl had a cast on her foot and was on crutches.

Mrs. Barber must have assessed the impending crisis with a rapid response time, because she immediately jumped into a defensive stance, throwing her body between the girl on crutches and the group of eighth graders, her arms raised and her head down, and blocked their path, narrowly averting a collision.

"Oh, sorry, Mrs. Barber," said the tallest of the eighth graders.

"Do watch where you're walking, boys," said Mrs. Barber.

Alex turned to look at Ava. Ava had seen it too.

"Defense?" asked Alex.

Ava nodded. "Blocker for sure," she said. "I'll go talk to her."

At lunch Ava was just unwrapping her peanut butter sandwich when her friend Jack Valdeavano appeared before her, panting slightly, his dark eyes sparkling.

Ava set down her sandwich. "Another recruit?" she asked him. She'd told Jack about her recruiting mission in math class earlier, and he'd been all over the idea of helping her scout talent.

Jack nodded. "Look over there. Ms. Nelson."

Ava looked. Ms. Nelson, a young seventh-grade math teacher, was weaving her way through the throng of chattering kids, holding two trays above her head to avoid the jostling crowds.

"Why is she carrying two trays?" asked Ava, watching as Ms. Nelson pivoted, weaved, and glided through the crowd, keeping the trays perfectly level the whole time. There was a cup of water on each of the two trays, and not so much as a drop sloshed out.

"I was behind her in the line," said Jack. "She

told me she was bringing lunch to Mrs. Hyde, because she's in a meeting that's running late."

Ava nodded, still watching Ms. Nelson with a glittering eye. She stood up. "A born flanker. I'll go talk to her. Nice work, JV."

"Thanks, Coach," said Jack with a wide grin.

It was startling to hear herself called Coach, but Ava didn't mind it either. *My dad would probably be proud,* she thought.

At the end of the day, Ava and Alex met up once again at their lockers.

"How'd it go with the recruiting today?" asked Alex.

Ava was tugging at her sports bag, which was jammed in at the bottom of her cluttered locker. "Pretty well," she said, finally wresting it free. "I still need some speed, though. I—"

Suddenly they heard the clatter of heels coming down the hall. Mrs. Monti, a science teacher, was tearing after a tiny brown mouse. "Make way!" she shouted, her high heels kicking up behind her, her lab coat flapping open. "Don't step on him!"

Kids leaped out of the way as the mouse scurried behind a trash can at the corner. Mrs. Monti scooped it up, cupping it gently between two perfectly manicured hands. "He got out of the cage somehow," she explained to the onlookers.

Ava looked at Alex. One of Alex's eyebrows shot up. "That was quite a show of speed," Ava said. "The woman's got wheels."

Alex rolled her eyes. "You sound exactly like Daddy," she said with a laugh.

After dinner that night, Mrs. Sackett knocked on Ava's door. Ava was lying on her bed, frowning down at her science textbook. Moxy was sprawled alongside her, lying on her back with her four paws in the air.

Moxy opened one eye when Mrs. Sackett appeared, and then hastily leaped to the floor. She knew Mrs. Sackett didn't approve of dogs on the beds.

"Honey, I just wanted to make sure everything is okay at school," said Mrs. Sackett. "You haven't mentioned anything about your science test, and I know that you and Luke were studying really hard together. Did it go okay?"

How does she always seem to know when I have a problem? Ava wondered. She set down her book. "Yeah, about that test. I did run into a little snag with it. We had a sub on Monday, and she didn't realize I was entitled to extra time, and I didn't get to finish it."

Mrs. Sackett frowned and started to say something.

"But don't worry," Ava added hastily. "I solved the problem myself." She told her mother everything that had happened.

"I'm really proud of the way you handled it," said Mrs. Sackett, patting Ava's leg. "That was very mature of you."

"And Mrs. Fowler just e-mailed me to say Mr. Cho sent her two new essay questions for me to answer," Ava continued. "So I'm trying to figure out what they might be. I get to finish the test tomorrow."

Her mom kissed her on the top of her head and left her to her studies.

Half an hour later, Ava sighed and put her book down. Moxy had jumped back up onto the bed after Mrs. Sackett had left, and Ava rubbed her dog's tummy, wishing she could stay more focused. Her mind kept wandering to the Powder Puff championship game the next day, and which teachers and students she would start with.

Alex popped her head in. "How's the studying going?"

"It's going," said Ava. "But I'm starting to have trouble concentrating. I'm just not good at absorbing a ton of information this quickly. My mind keeps wandering."

Alex came in and plopped down on the bed. Moxy shifted a little to give Alex better access to petting her tummy. "I bet you a million dollars they'll ask you to diagram a plant and an animal cell," she said. "Teachers love diagrams. And then I bet you the question will ask you to compare and contrast them, and maybe the other will be to describe the eukaryotic cell."

Ava nodded. "They had us compare and contrast plant and animal cells on the original test, but we didn't have to diagram them," she said. "Maybe I'll practice doing that."

"I practically guarantee it," said Alex with a smile.

"Hey, Al? By the way, I'm sorry I wasn't that supportive toward you with all the Powder Puff stuff. I get what a big deal it is. And you really played smart yesterday. You guys deserved to win."

Alex brightened. "You think so? That was a pretty cool lateral pass I made, huh?"

There she goes again with the lateral pass, Ava thought, smiling.

"Got to go choose my bow for tomorrow's game," said Alex. "I have it narrowed down to either an orange stripe or white with orange polka dots. Good luck studying."

CHAPTER ELEVEN

Friday at lunch Ava nervously reported to Mrs. Hyde's office for her test. But as soon as Mrs. Hyde put the two new questions down in front of her, Ava smiled and let out her breath. Alex had been right. The first question asked her to draw a plant and an animal cell diagram. The second question asked her to explain the difference between prokaryotic and eukaryotic cells. She silently thanked her sister and got to work. She had no trouble labeling the mitochondria and the ribosomes and the chloroplasts and the endoplasmic reticulum. The essay was easy too. She even finished at least five minutes before the bell rang, handed the test to Mrs. Hyde, and practically danced out of Mrs. Hyde's office.

Now she could concentrate on the big game today with an untroubled mind.

After her last class, she ran to her locker to collect her books before the pep rally, knowing she'd need to make a quick dash to football practice after it was over. When she walked out of the gym and onto the middle school football field a few minutes after the bell, things were already in full swing.

The seventh-grade student-faculty team stood on one sideline, wearing orange. The eighth-grade team was on the other sideline, wearing blue. The middle school band was playing a rousing, slightly out-of-tune version of the school song. But it was the two groups of seventh- and eighth-grade boys who attracted the most attention. They were dressed for cheering.

The seventh graders were wearing orange shirts that read TUFF ENOUGH FOR POWDER PUFF. Most wore jeans or gym shorts with their shirts, and most also had big bows in their hair. Ava laughed when she saw Jack, and then Corey and Xander, holding their orange pom-poms. Kal Tippett and Owen Rooney had painted their faces with tiger stripes.

"Hey, Ave!" called Jack, beckoning her over with one of his pom-poms. "How do I look?"

"Gorgeous," said Ava.

"You look pretty fly yourself," said Jack.

Coach had lent Ava one of his orange hats that said COACH on it. Wearing it made her feel so much more like a coach.

"Lindsey and Emily are going to coach us today," said Jack. "And Greg Fowler and Owen can actually do some tumbling. So be sure to watch our halftime performance."

"I wouldn't miss it for the world," said Ava.

"You'd better not, or I'll hit you with my pom-poms."

Mr. Kenerson blew his whistle to gather the two Powder Puff teams together. He was dressed in his black-and-white-striped officiating shirt. Ava joined her team.

Mrs. Fowler was wearing some sort of tennis skirt with her orange T-shirt. And her white tennis shoes looked all wrong. Mrs. Monti was decked out in a headband, sweatbands, and kneepads—the sort of paraphernalia that Ava had always thought cried "nonathlete." But Ava had seen what these teachers could do. She focused on Mr. Kenerson, who was reminding them of the rules.

"There must be at least five faculty members on the field at all times, for each team," he said, reading from his clipboard. "There is to be no unnecessary roughness or intentional tackling," he continued. "And that means you, Barbara Barber and Sheila Burleigh," he said, looking at the two teachers with a sly grin.

Mrs. Barber and Mrs. Burleigh both gave him a *who me?* look, and everyone laughed.

Ava felt someone elbow her and turned. It was Alex.

"Are you sure about these faculty members you chose?" Alex whispered out of the corner of her mouth. "Look at Mrs. Barber. She's wearing socks with pirates on them."

"I know," replied Ava, also in a whisper. "But it's all we have to work with. All we can do is our best."

Alex nodded grimly.

As the players walked onto the field, the seventh-grade boy cheerleaders lined up on the sideline and did their first cheer routine. Corey and Xander hoisted Jack up into the air. Jack leaped off their hands, did a pretty decent pike in the air, and landed in a sitting position on Xander and Corey's arms. The crowd cheered as Jack landed lightly on his feet and bowed. Ava rolled her eyes and grinned.

At halftime the game remained scoreless. *Not so much because the defense is so good,* Ava thought, *but more because the players on offense can't quite seem to coordinate the plays.* Once Ms. Nelson nearly scored a touchdown for the other team, but luckily, Mrs. Monti ran in from a diagonal and grabbed her flag before she could. The eighth graders protested about grabbing one's own teammate's flag, but Mr. Kenerson allowed it.

During the halftime show the boys performed a step routine, which was to be judged by a faculty panel. First the seventh-grade squad performed, and then the eighth grade. Alex and Ava stood side by side and watched. It was hard not to laugh, watching the seventh graders try to stay in step with one another. Owen and Greg performed a couple of tumbling stunts that were actually pretty impressive.

After the eighth-grade routine, the middle school band marched onto the field and played the school song. The crowd sang along with the music and then applauded wildly as they marched off again.

By now all the sixth graders had joined the rest of the fans in the stands. Their tug-of-war competition was over. Ava gazed at the bleachers, which were a sea of people—way more than showed up for the middle school football games. It seemed as though the entire middle school was here. She grinned. Maybe Alex had been right about this game being huge.

Ava gathered her team into a huddle. "Okay, Mrs. Fowler, now it's time for us to see some of that speed of yours," she said. "Try that stutter-step move we talked about. I don't think Mrs. Burleigh is as quick as you are."

Mrs. Fowler nodded intently.

"And Ms. Nelson, I think the best thing is for you to run deep crossing patterns, and—"

"What's a crossing pattern?" asked several people at the same time, including Ms. Nelson.

Ava passed a hand across her brow. "Sorry. Just run as fast as you can and turn around so Rosa can pass the ball to you. And then run in that direction." She pointed toward the opposite end zone.

"What about me?" demanded Kylie. "Owen and I have been doing a little practicing. I'm getting way better at catching the ball."

Ava looked at her thoughtfully. "Good to know, Ky," she said, grinning because Kylie's cheeks always turned a little pink whenever she talked about Owen. "I'll put you in as a receiver."

In the final ten minutes of the game, the eighth-grade team scored two quick touchdowns in succession. The score was 16–0.

Miraculously, Tessa Jones caught the kickoff without dropping it and tore down the field, her pink sneakers flying. Mrs. Barber blocked for her most of the way. Then Rosa ran it in for two extra points. The score was 16–8.

Ava watched as Jack and Greg performed several cartwheels, while Corey, Xander, and Logan Medina executed three spread-eagle jumps in perfect unison, their pom-poms high. She laughed. She was starting to understand more and more why this game was such a popular event. Behind the boys, she could see Lindsey and Emily trying not to laugh as they attempted to teach the "cheerleaders" some simple cheers.

Ava sent Annelise in for the kickoff. She'd shown some aptitude for it in the last game. Unfortunately, she kicked it out of bounds, so the eighth-grade team got it on their forty yard line.

"Uh-oh," said Alex. "Are we in trouble? That's

not very far to go. It doesn't seem fair of Mr. Kenerson to let them have the ball so close, just because Annelise had a little trouble with the kick."

"It's the rules, Al," said Ava. She turned to her defensive team. "Go in and stop them, guys," she said. "We're going to blitz."

Her team of defenders certainly looked tough and determined, with their cheeks swathed with eye black.

"We'll stop 'em, Coach," said Mrs. Barber.

The eighth-grade quarterback took the snap, but Mrs. Barber and Sydney Gallagher immediately bore down on her. Clearly rattled, she passed the ball backward to Ms. Peterson, the math teacher, who, momentarily confused, ran the wrong way toward her team's end zone. The eighth-grade fans on the sidelines bellowed at her to turn and go the other way, but it was too late. Mrs. Monti managed to grab Ms. Peterson's flag in her own end zone. The seventh-grade boy cheer squad went crazy.

The scoreboard flipped to 16–10.

Alex, who wasn't in the game at the moment, looked at Ava, totally perplexed. "She ran in the wrong direction, just like I did last game! But how did our team just score two points? What just happened?"

"It's called a safety," Ava explained. "If we tackle the other team—or grab their player's flag, in this case—in their own end zone, it's two points for us! Come on, kick return, team! We're receiving the ball! Get in there! We're only down by six! We have four minutes to tie up this game!"

Fortunately for the seventh-grade team, the eighth-grade team made a horrible kick. Tessa caught the kickoff at the fifty yard line but promptly fell down. The seventh-grade fan section roared with approval when she caught the ball and then groaned with frustration when she fell.

On second down and seven, Rosa, as quarterback, found Mrs. Fowler, who showed why she'd been a softball district champ as she caught the pass deftly at the thirty yard line. Mrs. Fowler dodged an eighth grader who was bearing down on her from the left, spun to the right, and zoomed down the field. The crowd went quiet in amazement for a few seconds as everyone watched her run. She coasted across the end line, a good five feet ahead of the opposing players trying to grab her flag.

Mr. Kenerson's arms shot upward. Touchdown.

The whole school roared. The score was tied, 16–16, with just twenty seconds left in the game. The clock stopped for their time-out.

"I think we should run it in," said Rosa to Ava.

Alex started to say something, but then appeared to decide not to. *Maybe, just maybe,* Ava thought, *she's adjusting to letting other people be in charge*.

"That's a good idea," Ava said. She didn't want to risk kicking, given Annelise's disastrous kickoff earlier.

"Someone stepped on my toe, and it really hurts," said Tessa. "I don't think I can play."

Ava gaped at her. "There are just twenty seconds left on the clock!" she said incredulously. "We need you in there!" This was not the sort of thing that happened in a real football game. She had to remind herself that this was Powder Puff.

"I'll go in for her," said Alex meekly.

Ava and Rosa exchanged looks. Rosa nodded.

"I mean—I don't have to," said Alex quickly. "It's up to you and Rosa. But if you need me to, I will."

Ava hesitated, but reminded herself that a

good coach should reward a player for being team-oriented. Even if that player was her twin sister, who really, really stunk at football. "Okay, Al. Win this one for us," she said.

The crowd grew quieter as the eighth-grade defenders lined up to face the seventh-grade extra point team, which now included Alex Sackett, in for the "injured" Tessa. Annelise hiked the ball to Rosa, who looked around quickly for an open player. But the eighth-grade team was providing excellent coverage, and Mrs. Burleigh was making a beeline for Rosa. In desperation, she sidearmed the ball to Kylie.

Kylie bobbled it. The ball shot out of her arms and up into the air.

Ava prayed.

The ball landed in the arms of a surprised Alex.

Ava held her breath.

Alex pulled it in and clutched it tight to her chest. With her head down, she barreled across the end line and fell, but she didn't let go of the ball. Just as Alex fell, an eighth grader snatched her flag and held it aloft.

Had she grabbed Alex's flag before Alex crossed the end line?

The crowd waited, holding its collective breath.

Mr. Kenerson stooped down to see where Alex had fallen. He stood up and turned toward the crowd.

His arms shot up. The conversion was good!

The seventh-grade team had won.

CHAPTER TWELVE

After the game, Emily and Lindsey ran up behind Alex and hooked their arms in hers. "That was so awesome, Alex!" said Emily.

"You were the star!" said Lindsey.

Alex beamed. It felt so good to have her friends paying attention to her again. "Thanks, you guys," she said. "It was kind of a lucky catch."

"You were in the right place at the right time," said Emily.

"We're sorry we were kind of ignoring you when you were on the other team," said Lindsey.

"I guess we just got a little caught up in the spirit of things," added Emily.

"Don't apologize," said Alex generously. "I'm

just glad the seventh-grade team won. Especially because there's going to be an ice cream social and the eighth graders have to serve us!" She giggled.

"We'll see you tonight at the high school game then," said Lindsey. "We have to run off to cheerleading practice."

"Save me a seat!" called Alex. She headed inside to the gym. As class president, she was on the decoration committee for the Homecoming dance the next night. She wasn't totally in charge—the eighth graders had been allowed to select the color scheme, which had been hard for her, because she was great at decorating and had an excellent color sense. Luckily, they'd chosen silver and blue. And they'd been highly receptive to Alex's ideas for some of the decorations, so that was a relief. She wasn't sure she could handle taking a backseat on something important twice in one week!

At the Friday night game the Tigers narrowly squeaked out a victory over the Western Longhorns, one of their most challenging opponents. Ava, sitting between Kylie and Jack, leaped to her feet along with the rest of the Ashland crowd and double-high-fived everyone in the immediate vicinity of her seat. Everyone else was doing the same thing. Ava was relieved. Coach had been very worried about this game.

"Does this mean we're going to the play-offs?" yelled Kylie above the din.

"Yes!" replied Ava.

Kylie let out a whoop. "Now we have double reason to celebrate!" she said. "First the seventh-grade Powder Puff victory, and now AHS. Let's go to Sal's!"

Ava and Jack agreed, and the three headed down to join the big clump of middle school kids getting ready to walk over to their favorite hangout.

"Hey," said Ava, nudging Jack with her elbow. "Thanks for your cheering support during the game today."

Jack grinned. "You're welcome, Coach."

Kids had been calling Ava "Coach" all afternoon, ever since the Powder Puff victory. It definitely felt weird to be called what she called her own father. But weird in a good way.

"I'm not going to lie," Jack continued. "I

thought our halftime dance routine was pretty awesome. I totally thought we were better than the eighth-grade team. They didn't even point their toes."

Ava laughed. "I hope someone recorded it," she said. "Because I was pretty focused on coaching my team. But I did notice how pretty your orange hair bow looked."

Jack patted his hair gently, first with one hand, then with the other. "Thanks. My hair may never look that good again."

Alex waved to her twin as Ava, Kylie, and Jack walked into Sal's half an hour later. Alex was sitting between Lindsey and Emily in a booth for six people, but this time she felt like she was part of the group. Across from them were Annelise, Tessa, and Rosa. Ava gave Alex a thumbs-up and with her eyes told her twin that it was okay that Alex was sitting with a different group. Alex and Ava had always been able to communicate silently with each other—their creepy twin thing, as Tommy referred to it. She could see that Ava didn't care a bit if Lindsey and Emily were no longer paying much attention to her, now that Powder Puff was over. Alex was pretty sure Ava not only didn't mind, but flat-out preferred it that way.

Alex turned her attention to the conversation before her, which had suddenly shifted to the dance. Alex had been at school most of the afternoon, twisting paper flowers and hanging strings of lights, but they'd been mostly mindless tasks, so she'd had plenty of time to obsess about her outfit, and even more so about what her *mother* was going to wear to the dance. It still seemed so bizarre that middle school kids were supposed to bring their moms to Homecoming. And Alex hadn't even had a second to discuss it with her mother!

"What's your mum going to look like?" Annelise asked Rosa.

"Oh, you know. Not too flashy, but not too plain, either," replied Rosa.

"Mine's going to light up!" said Emily, her eyes dancing. "We found some battery-powered LED lights that sparkle. They're awesome."

"Your mum is going to *sparkle*?" Alex blurted out. She still couldn't believe these girls were more interested in what their mothers were going to wear than what they themselves would.

"Sure!" said Emily. "I think it's going to look pretty great with my pink dress."

"But does she mind wearing sparkles?" persisted Alex.

There was a confused silence.

"Does *who* mind?" asked Emily.

"Your mum."

"My *mom*?"

"Yes, your mom."

"Who said anything about my *mom*?"

Now Alex was truly confused. "Didn't you just say your mom was going to be wearing sparkles and coming with you to Homecoming?"

There was another momentary silence, and then suddenly everyone at the table erupted in giggles. Everyone except Alex. And then, because they didn't seem to be the mean kind of giggles, Alex laughed weakly along with them.

Rosa spoke first. "Alex, I think we have some explaining to do," she said, not unkindly. "We're talking about *mums*, not our moms."

"I thought you were suddenly speaking with English accents," said Alex.

More giggles around the table.

"Mums are a Texas tradition," said Emily. "They're like—what would you call them, Lindz? Corsages?"

"Giant corsages," said Lindsey, nodding.

"So they're these giant corsages that girls wear to Homecoming. They're made of ribbons and crafty stuff, and usually we make them ourselves, or our moms help us, although in high school the boys are supposed to make them for their dates."

"Oh," said Alex, suddenly feeling faint. "I guess maybe I should go home and get started on mine."

"Mine took forever for us to make," said Annelise.

"Yeah, mine, too," said Tessa.

Alex plunked some money down on the table for her soda and scooted out of the booth. "I better make Ava come with me," she said. "She'll need one too."

Her friends wished her good luck, and she scurried over to tell Ava they had to go home right this instant.

Even Ava seemed alarmed by the news Alex delivered to her, and she agreed to go home with Alex right away.

"A mum?" Ava kept muttering under her breath as the two girls speed-walked home. "Whoever heard of a *mum*?"

They reached home half an hour later. Thankfully, Alex saw her mother's car in the driveway. "Mom! Mom!" she yelled as they flung open the kitchen door.

Moxy scrambled to her feet in alarm and ran up to the girls, sniffing worriedly to be sure they were unhurt.

Seconds later Mrs. Sackett came flying down the stairs, her toothbrush still in her hand, her mouth full of toothpaste. "Wuh! Wuhs wrong!" she said, her voice panicky.

The door to Coach's study banged open, and he was in the kitchen a second behind his wife, eyes wide.

"It's the dance tomorrow!" said Alex, panting heavily from the run home. "We need these things called mums. They're like giant, weird corsages that only people from Texas know about."

Mrs. Sackett collapsed with relief against the kitchen counter, then turned to spit the toothpaste into the sink. “I thought some disaster had happened,” she said, rinsing her toothbrush.

“It *is* a disaster,” said Alex. “Ava and I just heard about them tonight. Evidently they take hours and hours to make.”

“Now, Al,” said Coach. “Let’s not panic here.”

“Panic?” said Alex, her voice climbing. “Of *course* I’m panicked!”

“Even I’m mildly panicked,” said Ava.

“Panicked about what?” asked Tommy. In their haste, Alex and Ava had left the kitchen door open, and Tommy stood in the doorway.

“Alex and I are supposed to wear these weird, giant corsages to the dance tomorrow night,” Ava explained. “And we didn’t even know what they *were* until tonight.”

“You guys need to learn to chill,” said Tommy, moving to the refrigerator. He opened it up and inspected the contents.

“Now that’s enough, T,” said Coach. “This stuff is important when you’re in middle school. Right, Laura? Laur?”

“Mom,” said Alex sternly. “I don’t think *laughing* about this situation is *appropriate* here. This is a social *disaster* for Ava and me.”

"I'm sorry, honey," said Mrs. Sackett. "I wasn't laughing *at* you. I have something to show you. Be right back."

Alex and Ava watched Tommy pull out a stack of cold cuts, mustard, and lettuce, balancing everything precariously on a pickle jar and holding the stack in place with his chin as he kicked the door closed and carried his supplies to the counter.

Mrs. Sackett was back a minute later, holding something behind her back. Then, with a flourish, she brought her hands out and held up two items for the girls to see.

Alex gasped. Even Ava looked impressed.

"You made these for us?" Alex asked. She stared down at the huge, glittering mums, like oversize versions of first-place ribbons at a state fair, except that they were bedecked with sequins, curled silver and gold ribbons, and even fluffy white feathers. "These are totally awesome!" she said breathlessly.

Ava was looking at the mums dubiously, as though she couldn't imagine wearing such a thing. But that was Ava, of course, the girl who wouldn't be caught dead with *lip gloss* on.

"It was going to be a surprise, tomorrow,"

said Mrs. Sackett. “I was talking to April Cahill at Ave’s game last week, and she told me all about the tradition. She helped me make them.”

Tommy piled turkey and Swiss cheese onto the bottom half of his sandwich. As he picked up the jar of pickles, he cocked his head sideways at the mums. “Those are some seriously weird decorations,” he pronounced, and turned back to his sandwich construction. “Middle school is one strange place.”

“Yeah, well, Lindsey told me that here in the great state of Texas, in high school, the boys make the mums for their dates,” Alex said. She turned to her mother. “So Mom, how do we hang the mums—”

A spoon clattered to the counter. The rest of the Sacketts turned to look at Tommy.

“Tommy? How come your face just went all pale?” asked Ava. “Tommy? You okay?”

“I’m guessing he didn’t know about the mums either,” said Alex.

“Texting . . . Luke,” croaked Tommy. His thumbs flew around his keyboard. Then he stood, waiting, his phone in his hand.

His phone beeped. The rest of the Sacketts waited.

Tommy read the text, and then lowered his phone carefully down onto the counter. "Luke says I need a mim or a ma'am or whatever it's called too," he said hoarsely.

"Don't worry," said Alex. "I'm sure Mom's thought about that, too. Haven't you, Mom?"

Now it was Mrs. Sackett's turn to go pale. "Oh, sweetie. I had no idea. I never thought—I never dreamed—"

Alex resisted the urge to say *I told you so*, but she couldn't resist looking smugly at her brother. After all, he'd just been making fun of the whole mum tradition. But the expression on Tommy's face was just too pathetic to bear. Plus, he really, really needed a haircut, but that was something to focus on later. Her mind raced.

Coach looked uneasily from his wife to his son. "Is this something we can fix?" he asked. "You know crafty stuff isn't my strength, but . . ."

Alex snapped into action. "We can do it together," she said. "I'll go get Mom's supply bin. Tommy, you go to the attic and bring down the box of Christmas decorations. I know they're there because I carried that box up there on moving day. Ave—maybe you should call Kylie and ask for some suggestions. Her sister is super popular at the high school, and she'll for sure be able to give us some guidance about making one for a high school girl."

Ava whipped out her phone. "I'm on it," she said.

Coach smiled. "Then I'll make some cookies," he said. "Come on, Sacketts. Let's show what a little teamwork can accomplish."

CHAPTER THIRTEEN

Saturday morning, Ava was still savoring her team's easy victory over the Cleary Chargers when Alex appeared near the fence and beckoned her over. Ava knew that look on her sister's face. It meant business. She dropped her big duffel bag near the bench and trotted up to speak to Alex.

"Nice game," said Alex, although Ava could readily see that her sister had long since put the Ashland Middle School victory behind her. "Can you come home with us? We need to figure out what we're both wearing to the dance."

"I can't think too hard about that," said Ava. "Making Tommy's mum last night took a lot out of me. I was just going to wear a shirt. And maybe some pants."

Alex raised a hand to her brow and looked deeply pained.

"What?" said Ava. "Al, the term 'snappy casual' means nothing. I'm sure there will be kids in jeans and jerseys."

"But not the girls," said Alex. "May I remind you that even though you play football, you're still a girl?"

"That ridiculous mum is going to cover most of whatever I'm wearing anyway," Ava said.

Alex continued to stare at Ava. She knew her sister was weakening.

Sure enough, Ava sighed. "Okay, you win. I'll come home with you, and you can help me find something to wear."

Alex smiled. "I knew you'd come around," she said. "I've also convinced Tommy to let me shape his hair a little so he'll look great for his Homecoming tonight. His curls are totally out of control."

Later that afternoon Ava stood in front of Alex's full-length mirror and studied her reflection in the mirror. How had she allowed Alex to talk her into wearing a dress? She knew how. When Alex was determined to make something happen, it was practically useless to resist. She looked fine. Just not like herself.

Downstairs in the kitchen, she could hear Alex and Tommy returning from their errand. When even Coach had agreed that Tommy's hair was beyond unruly, Tommy had tried to make an appointment at a haircut place, but everywhere in town was booked. So he'd finally relented and told Alex she could do it. Alex had talked him into splitting the cost of a pair of haircutting clippers at the beauty supply shop. She'd convinced him that in the long run, he'd be saving piles of money by not having to pay for salon haircuts.

Ava turned around and looked back over her shoulder. The dress she'd borrowed from Alex was plain, a pale purple shade. The hem had a little flouncy ruffle. She twirled around and watched it spin. She had to admit, she didn't look stupid or anything. She wondered what Jack would say when he saw her. Then she wondered if she'd have to wear that weird mum around her neck for the entire evening. The thing was enormous.

Then she heard Tommy howl. "Uh-oh," she said to her own reflection, and raced out of the room.

Ava found Tommy sitting on a kitchen stool, his shirt off, a towel draped around his neck. Alex stood behind him, looking quietly stricken. Tommy had picked up the hand mirror and was staring into it.

"It's not my fault you moved!" Alex said.

"You almost cut my ear off!" said Tommy. "But instead you gave me half a Mohawk! Ave! Look at me!"

Ava looked. Sure enough, a large tuft of brown curls was on the floor at Tommy's feet. Above his right ear, a patch of hair was distinctly . . . missing. Ava could see the pale, shiny skin of his scalp.

Alex, still holding the clippers, had gone white. "I might have used the wrong attachment," she said in a tiny voice.

"What are you going to do now?" asked Ava, staring at Tommy with horrified fascination.

"I have to wear a *hat* to Homecoming!" Tommy said bitterly. "And I can't take it off for a month!"

"Let me go get my art supplies," suggested

Alex. "I could maybe color in the bald spot over your ear with brown marker."

"I'm not going to go to Homecoming with brown marker on my head," said Tommy through clenched teeth.

"No. We're not going to panic," said Alex. "I'm pretty sure I saw a video about how to fix haircuts. Let me just go do some research."

"No way," said Tommy, and his voice sounded steely. "I'll call Cassie."

"What is she going to do?" asked Alex.

"She actually *knows* how to cut hair," said Tommy. "She has four brothers, and she told me she cuts their hair all the time."

This is an interesting twist, thought Ava. Tommy was so private about his dating life. Now they'd actually have a chance to meet the girl he was going to the dance with!

"So why didn't you ask her to do it in the first place?" asked Ava, genuinely curious.

"Because (a) I thought my hair looked fine the way it was," said Tommy. "And (b), because I don't know the girl very well, so I'm not *exactly* in the habit of asking her to cut my *hair*. That's a rather *personal* request. But this is an emergency." He texted her.

Alex backed away and leaned against the counter, an anxious look on her face.

Ava ran upstairs and changed out of her dress. She threw on a T-shirt and running shorts, and then returned to the kitchen.

The three of them waited, listening to the ticking of the kitchen clock and to Tommy's fingers, drumming on the kitchen table. Ava tried not to stare at the tuft of hair on the floor. She didn't dare meet Alex's gaze either.

After a while they heard a car pull up, and then there was a tap at the kitchen door. Ava sprang to open it.

A pretty girl stepped in. The first thing Ava noticed was her hair—it was raven black and pulled back into a casual ponytail. She had light-brown skin and huge, dark eyes. And she was wearing a New England Patriots jersey! Ava's mouth fell open. She forgot to say hello.

"This is Cassie," said Tommy abruptly. "Cassie, this is my sister Ava, and her evil twin, Alex, the one who just shaved off half my hair."

Cassie smiled at the girls and then turned to Tommy. Ava could see her dark eyes dancing with merriment, but she managed not to laugh out loud. "Oh, my, my," she said, shaking her head as she looked at the troublesome patch of short hair above his ear.

"Can you fix it?" croaked Tommy.

"I definitely think that this is fixable," she replied. She rummaged through the clipper attachments and selected one. "Come watch, Alex. I'll show you how we're going to blend in what's, er, not there anymore. It will look okay, T, I promise."

Alex seemed grateful to be invited by Cassie to watch.

Ava stepped out of the way, but she remained in the kitchen, fascinated by what Cassie was wearing. A football jersey! And for Ava's favorite team!

Ava scrutinized the way Cassie lightly touched Tommy's shoulders as she examined his bald patch. And she'd called Tommy "T." That sounded so—girlfriendish. Was Cassie his actual girlfriend? Was she wearing one of Tommy's jerseys? Ava prided herself on not being nosy, the way Alex usually was, but she couldn't help herself. She had to know. "Um—are you a Patriots fan?" she asked Cassie.

Cassie was about to turn on the clippers, but she paused to answer. "My uncle's family lives in

Connecticut," she explained. "So yeah, I've been a Pats fan all my life. It doesn't always go over well around here." She laughed.

Ava nodded, enthralled. Tommy had found the perfect woman!

CHAPTER FOURTEEN

Both the middle school and the high school dances started at seven p.m. that night, so Mrs. Sackett insisted on taking a group picture of the three Sackett kids all dressed up. Ava was the first to come downstairs.

"Wow," said Coach. "Is this our Ava?"

"Don't embarrass her, Michael," said Mrs. Sackett, smacking his arm playfully. "Or she might run back upstairs and put on a football jersey. Honey, you look beautiful."

Ava felt like a dope. The dress she'd borrowed from Alex wasn't too uncomfortable—the material had a little stretch to it, so she could move reasonably freely—but this bizarre mum!

Her mom had added a loop around the top so that she could wear it around her neck. The long ribbons trailed almost to her ankles. "Do I have to wear this thing all night?" she asked.

Coach and her mom looked at each other. Mrs. Sackett raised her hands in a helpless gesture. "When in Texas, do as the Texans do," she said. "So just see what the other girls at the dance do with theirs, and follow their cue."

Tommy was the next one down. He wore a black suit and a fashionably narrow striped tie. It was strange to Ava to see his curly hair cropped short, but she conceded that he looked pretty good. And Cassie had done a nice job camouflaging the almost-bald spot that Alex had created. You could only see it if you looked closely. Cassie had left the sides a little long and had shown him how to glue the hair back and over the bare place with some of Alex's hair gel. With his hair slicked back and his elegant outfit, he actually looked kind of like a movie star, Ava thought.

"Luke's going to be here any minute," said Tommy. He picked up the mum they'd all made for Cassie, stared down at it, and shook his head, perplexed. "I don't think I have time for a picture."

"Yes, you do," said Mrs. Sackett firmly.

"Alex!" all four of them yelled at the same time.

Several seconds ticked by. They heard a muffled "Coming!" from upstairs, and then Alex's door opened and closed and she appeared at the top of the stairs.

Alex had finally decided on a shimmery silver shirt with a halter neckline over a short, twirling black skirt, and clunky black wedge sandals. She'd pulled her hair back into a dramatic, twisty high knot. She looked extremely glamorous, Ava thought, although the huge mum around her neck was a little distracting.

"All right. Let's take this picture, Mom. Quick," said Tom, as Alex finished drifting down the stairs like an old-fashioned movie star.

The three stood in front of the couch, with Tommy in the middle, an arm around each sister. Moxy insisted on being in the picture too and flopped down in front of them. Which worked out fine, because all three of them laughed at that, just as Mrs. Sackett snapped the picture.

There was a honk in the driveway.

"That's Luke. Gotta go," said Tommy, picking up the mum again. "Have fun, dudes," he said.

"Do you forgive me?" Alex called after him.

"Ask me in about eleven years," his voice called back.

"We need to go now too," said Alex, glancing at the clock over the mantel. "We're supposed to meet the whole gang in front of the school so we can walk in together."

Coach picked up his keys. "At your service, ladies," he said, and gestured gallantly toward the door.

Alex linked arms with Emily as they walked into the gym. In a way, she was glad she didn't have a real date. It was fun to go with all her friends. The only two people in her group who had ended up officially going as a couple were Lindsey and Corey.

All the girls had on their mums when Alex and Ava joined up with them, and Alex was relieved to see that the mums she and Ava were wearing fell just about in the middle of the pack in terms of elaborateness. She silently thanked her mother for the trillionth time.

They all purchased a raffle ticket as they

entered, at Annelise's insistence. "The sixth graders organize the raffle every year," she said, "There are, like, ten different prizes, and some of them are super awesome."

The gym looked amazing, Alex was thrilled to see. All that work had paid off. The place was transformed. The rotating silver mirror ball they'd rented (that had been Alex's idea) cast a thousand points of swirling white lights around the room. The effect was magical. The DJ was up on the stage, and the music was just the right volume. The song ended and a new one came on—a super-popular song that made everyone immediately start tapping their feet or nodding their heads.

"Come on!" said Emily. "Let's dance!"

She lifted her mum off from around her head and dumped it onto the nearest table. Alex did the same. Out of the corner of her eye she saw Corey and Lindsey dancing together and felt a tiny pang of jealousy. But it soon passed. Surrounded by Emily, Rosa, and Annelise, with Ava and Kylie nearby, Alex finally felt like she belonged.

Ava was immensely relieved when Kylie told her she could take off her mum almost as soon as they got to the dance. Kylie's mum was full of brightly colored feathers and beads. They dumped theirs together in an out-of-the-way corner near the portable basketball hoop.

It took Ava's eyes a few minutes to adjust to the spectacle in front of her. Alex had been blathering away about the silver ball the seventh-grade class had rented for the evening, and Ava had to admit that the effect was pretty awesome. She was beginning to be able to identify people in the dim, lavender-tinted glow flecked with tiny points of white light. There was Ms. Nelson, talking to Mr. Kenerson. There was Mrs. Monti, standing in towering high-heeled sandals, tapping her toe in time to the beat.

"Hey, Coach!" said a girl Ava didn't know, passing by with several other seventh graders.

"Coach! Nice dress!" said another.

At first Ava didn't acknowledge these greetings, but after the fourth person said "Coach," she realized they were addressing *her*.

"Look! There's Mrs. Fowler!" shouted Kylie to Ava over the music.

Sure enough, Mrs. Fowler seemed to be

making a beeline for them. She was beaming.

"Ava! I was going to wait until Monday to tell you, but I was just too excited not to tell you now—you got twelve out of fourteen points on both your essays! Your test grade has risen to a ninety! I'm so proud of you!"

Ava gasped. That was one of the best grades she'd gotten all year!

Kylie clapped her on the back. "Awesome job, Coach!"

Ava grinned. She kind of didn't mind this new nickname. "I can't wait to tell Alex!" she said.

The place was so crowded that Ava didn't manage to find her sister until just before they were going to announce the raffle winners. When Ava told her about her science grade, Alex gave her a huge hug, and Ava beamed.

"You know what prize I'm dying to win?" Alex said. "The day of beauty at the Belle Visage salon. That would be so totally awesome." She clutched her ticket stub and closed her eyes as though trying to will the principal, Ms. Farmen, to read her number.

"First off—the winner will receive three batting lessons with former major league batting champ Derek Rivera!" said Ms. Farmen. Most of the boys in the room adopted the closed-eyes praying posture Alex had just done. "And the winner is—Alex Sackett!"

Ava and Alex both gasped as the room erupted with the collective groans of disappointed non-winners, a smattering of laughter—but not mean laughter—from people who knew Alex, but mostly a warm round of applause. Alex laughed too and waved as she headed up to receive her prize in the form of a white envelope. Then Ms. Farmen was on to the next prize.

Alex rejoined Ava, and the two stood side by side, listening to Ms. Farmen read off a few more raffle prizes. "I never win anything," said Alex, "and now I get a total jock prize." She shrugged. "Maybe it's fate telling me to be more athletic," she said with a laugh. "Remember my lateral pass?"

"I sure do," said Ava with mock enthusiasm. Then she laughed too. "I never win anything either."

"And the winner is—*Ava* Sackett!"

Ava jumped as Ms. Farmen called out her name. She'd won a prize too? "Wait! What did I win?" she asked Alex over her shoulder as she started toward the stage.

"The makeover," Alex said, laughing. "Fate has spoken once again!"

Ava took the envelope from Ms. Farmen and turned to walk back toward Alex. The applause turned into a chant, which started low and then grew in volume: "Coach! Coach! Coach! Coach! Coach!"

Ava couldn't help but laugh, giddily, although she blushed from the attention.

"How ironic is it that I won a sports prize and you won a makeup prize?" Alex said to her when Ava returned to her sister's side.

Ava grinned. "May the best twin win," she said.

"Better."

"Huh?"

"May the *better* twin win," said Alex.

"Whatever," said Ava, and she grabbed Alex's hand and dragged her back to the dance floor.

Ready for more ALEX AND AVA?

Here's a sneak peek at the next book in the It Takes Two series:

Are You Thinking What I'm Thinking?

"I knew it," Alex Sackett declared. "I just knew it!"

"Knew what?" Ella Sanchez asked.

"That it was going to rain," Alex said. "It's pouring." She pointed toward the huge windows bordering Ashland Middle School's front door.

Ella peered through the rain-splattered glass. "Wow. It really is. Who knew?"

"I did!" Alex cried. "I sensed it this morning. I had this cute outfit planned, very nautical. Navy-and-white-striped top, navy pants, and my new red suede ballet flats. But I changed to a sweat-shirt and sneakers. Ava said I was nuts, because the sun was shining when we left the house."

"So she didn't change her outfit too?" Ella asked, pulling her dark hair into a ponytail.

"Hello? Have you met my twin sister?" Alex asked with a laugh. "She was already wearing jeans and a sweatshirt. Ava wears the same outfit practically every day, rain or shine."

Ella shook her head. "I don't have any classes with Ava. Why doesn't she do debate club with us?"

"It's not really her thing," Alex replied. She and Ella had just left the after-school meeting of the debate club. Although they'd gotten to know each other a little when they were both running for seventh-grade class president, they weren't close friends. But after watching Ella outdebate an eighth grader on why America needs a female president, Alex knew that would change. Especially because Ella had been really nice to Alex when Alex won the election.

Alex loved debate club. She loved sharing ideas and talking in front of a group. But Ava didn't—she loved sports. And she was good at them too. She was the only girl on the Ashland Tiger Cubs football team.

"Any sign of the late bus?" Ella asked.

Alex pressed her nose to the glass. The wind caused the trees to sway and the rain to pelt sideways. "Nothing yellow out there," she reported. "No bus yet."

Boom!

Alex jumped at the loud clap. Her eyes widened as a jagged streak of lightning slashed through the sky.

Ella squealed. "So cool! I love thunderstorms."

Alex bit her lip and tried to slow her thudding heart. She didn't think the storm was cool. Far from it.

Her family was still new to Texas. They had moved here over the summer from Massachusetts so her dad could coach the high school football team. Before a scary tornado hit a few weeks back, Alex had never been in a tornado. It had been horrible. She and Ava had to take cover in their bathtub!

She really hoped she wouldn't be in a second one.

Alex's eyes darted between the storm outside and the clock over the main office door. The bus was supposed to be there soon.

More kids gathered to wait, and snippets of their conversations swirled around her.

"Mr. Antonucci is giving a social studies test tomorrow."

"Have you seen that new app?"

". . . and then my mother said . . ."

Even with all the kids and noise, a lonely feeling suddenly overcame her. She wished Ava were by her side, like she had been during the last storm.

But Ava was at football practice in the gym. Sports let out after clubs, and the special sports bus left after the late bus. Ava would be on that bus.

Should I wait for Ava? Alex wondered.

She debated finding an excuse to stay at school longer so she could ride the bus with her sister. Maybe she could talk to Ms. Palmer about student council plans. But then she remembered she had seen Ms. Palmer leave before she went into debate club.

Stop it, she scolded herself. No one else seemed to be scared by this storm. It probably wasn't a big deal. She should just get on the late bus without Ava.

Think logically. She liked logic and facts and figures. *Not every storm is a tornado,* she reminded herself.

Alex flattened her palm against the window and peered out. The sky had grown dark.

Another crash of thunder boomed. The lightning flashed so close, it illuminated her hand.

Alex stifled a shriek.

This isn't about logic, she thought. This was about fear.

She really wished Ava was here to ride the bus home with her.

At that moment, in the window's reflection, Alex saw double. Green eyes like hers, pale skin with light freckles like hers, and curly, chocolate-brown hair like hers. Except this girl's hair was cropped to her chin, while Alex's fell past her shoulders.

"Ava!" Alex cried, and whirled around. She'd wished for her twin sister, and now she was here. A shiver ran down Alex's spine.

"Are you okay?" Ava asked. She hoisted her backpack onto her left shoulder and tilted her head at her twin.

"I'm fine . . . I'm totally fine," Alex said. She let out the breath she hadn't realized she'd been holding. "What are you doing here?"

"Coach Kenerson called practice early," Ava explained. "Because of the rain. I'm taking the late bus with you."

"That's so strange—" Alex began.

"The bus is here!" Ella called.

"Come on! Let's run for it," Ava said. She

headed out the door with the crowd of kids, and Alex followed.

As they sprinted through the sheets of rain, Alex grabbed her sister's hand. Together they boarded the bus, dripping puddles down the aisle as they made their way toward the back.

They slid into the seat behind Corey O'Sullivan and Jack Valdeavano. Raindrops fell from Corey's red hair. With a mischievous look, he gave his head an aggressive shake, spraying the twins.

"Gross! What are you, a wet dog?" Ava cried.

"Top dog," he boasted. "I'm your quarterback, remember? The star of the Tiger Cubs?"

"Conceited much?" Alex teased. Corey wasn't actually conceited, but he did have a great throwing arm and, as far as Alex was concerned, an even better smile. She wondered if he'd had braces before they moved here or if he'd been born with such an awesome grin.

"Just telling it like it is," Corey joked, puffing out his chest.

"It's so sad. The rain got into his brain," Jack said.

"From all the holes in his head," Ava added with a grin.

"Score!" Jack held up his hand. Ava slapped

his palm. Corey and Alex collapsed into giggles.

Ava continued to joke with Corey and Jack as the bus pulled out of the school parking lot. Ava played football with Corey and hung out with Jack a lot, shooting hoops at the nearby park. She had an easy way with boys that Alex envied—without Ava around, Alex wouldn't have known what to say to Jack and Corey.

The bus's headlights cut through the storm as it turned down another street.

Thunder boomed in the distance. The rain drumming against the bus's roof made Alex's skin tingle.

"It's spooky out there," she said.

"Spooky is good," Jack said. "We need to make next weekend spooky. But with no rain."

"What's next weekend?" Ava asked.

"Halloween," Alex answered. "Right, you're talking about Halloween?"

"Not just Halloween," Corey said. "Lindsey's party."

"It's going to be epic," Jack agreed.

Alex nodded, but her brain was spinning. Lindsey Davis was having a party? How could she not know this? Weren't she and Lindsey close friends?

"Is it a costume party?" Ava asked.

"Is there any other kind for Halloween?" Corey asked. "I helped Lindz come up with all these wacky categories. Makes My Little Sister Cry. Weirdest Superhero. Most Likely to Get the Most Likes. The winning costumes get prizes."

Alex chewed her lip. *It's not strange that Corey knows all this about the party,* she told herself. *Lindsey and Corey are going out. Still . . . could* I *really not be invited?*

"Lindsey told us about it at lunch," Jack said.

Aha! Alex had missed lunch today to make signs for the student council car wash. "So are we all invited?"

She had to ask, just to be extra sure.

"I think you're the one with water in the brain," Corey said to Alex. "Of course we're all invited. Practically the whole seventh grade is invited!"

Alex nodded, as if she already knew this.

"I heard Sloane promised to make food for the party," Jack offered. Lindsey's older sister Sloane had graduated high school and was now in culinary school.

"And I'm going to eat it all!" Corey cried. "Sloane makes these insane pumpkin cupcakes with cream filling. Lindsey should do a cupcake-eating contest. I'd win."

"I want to win one of the costume prizes," Ava said.

"Me too," Alex agreed. "I always plan my Halloween costume in July. I have a really original one this year."

"Not me," Ava said. "I always wait until the last minute. But I came up with an idea this morning."

"So what are you guys going to be?" Jack asked.

"A Spelling Bee!" Alex and Ava said at the same time.

Alex met Ava's surprised gaze. Another shiver ran down her spine.

"Together?" Jack asked.

"No, not together." Alex pulled her fingers through her damp hair. She didn't recall ever telling Ava her idea. How could they have come up with the exact same costume?

"What is a Spelling Bee?" Corey asked.

"I'm going to wearing a cute bumblebee outfit. Yellow and black with wings and a stinger," Alex explained. "Then I'm going to attach letters from the alphabet to my bee body. Get it? Spelling Bee?"

Corey groaned. "Leave it to the Sackett twins to make Halloween complicated. Ever hear of a witch or a ghost?"

"Boring," Ava said. "Alex and I definitely don't do boring."

"And you're going to make the same bee costume as Alex?" Jack asked Ava.

Ava shrugged. "The idea just randomly popped into my mind. But yeah, sure. It would be funny if we were twin bees." Ava laughed, and Corey and Jack joined in.

"*Spelling* bees," Alex corrected her.

But already her mind was spinning. In the past, she and Ava had always chosen costumes that were totally different. Once she'd been a princess and Ava had been a dragon slayer. The year she was a bunny, Ava was a dinosaur. Last year Alex had gone as an angel and Ava had decided on Halloween morning to go as a devil. So why had they all of a sudden picked the same costume?

Belle Payton isn't a twin herself, but she does have twin brothers! She spent much of her childhood in the bleachers reading—er, cheering them on—at their football games. Though she left the South long ago to become a children's book editor in New York City, Belle still drinks approximately a gallon of sweet tea a week and loves treating her friends to her famous homemade mac-and-cheese. Belle is the author of many books for children and tweens, and is currently having a blast writing two sides to each It Takes Two story.

More books about Alex and Ava?
That's **TWO** good to be true!

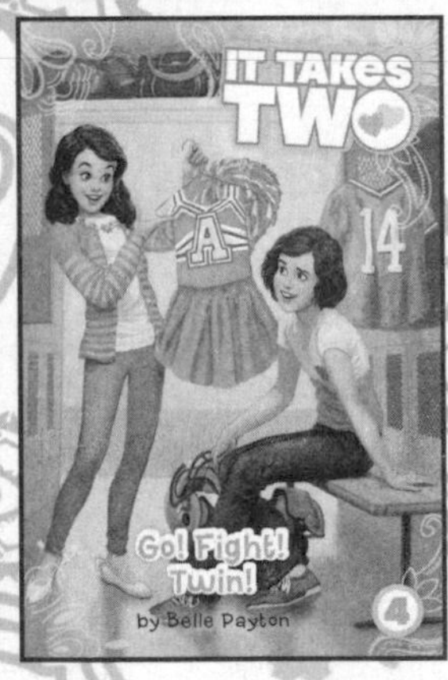

Available at your favorite store!

EBOOK EDITIONS ALSO AVAILABLE

ItTakesTwoBooks.com • Published by Simon Spotlight • Kids.SimonandSchuster.com

KEEP UP WITH TWINS ALEX AND AVA
at ItTakesTwoBooks.com

You'll find chapter excerpts,
downloadable activities, and more!